Gytha's Message

Emma Leslie Church History Series

LEOFRIC AND GYTHA AT THE CONVENT DOOR

Page 5

EMMA LESLIE CHURCH HISTORY SERIES

Gytha's Message

A Tale of Saxon England

BY

EMMA LESLIE

Illustrated by
C. J. STANILAND R.I.

Salem Ridge Press
Emmaus, Pennsylvania

Originally Published
1885
Blackie & Son, Limited

Republished 2006
Historical notes added in 2007
Salem Ridge Press LLC
4263 Salem Drive
Emmaus, Pennsylvania 18049

www.salemridgepress.com

Hardcover ISBN: 978-1-934671-11-5
Softcover   ISBN: 978-0-9776786-4-8

PUBLISHER'S NOTE

Gytha's Message contains several significant and dramatic historical events; however, the author, Emma Leslie, uses these events as a backdrop to address important questions about the Providence of God and the purpose of Christians in the world—questions that confront Christians to this day. The author also gives us many examples of positive character qualities such as patience, submission, courage and self-sacrifice.

I pray that as you read *Gytha's Message* you will be encouraged by the simple yet profound lessons taught by a loving God to His faithful servant, Gytha.

Daniel Mills

October, 2007

HISTORICAL NOTES

By the fifth century A.D., the weakened Roman Empire was no longer able to maintain control of the island of Britain. In addition, many of the native Britons had migrated to the European continent, settling along the coast, including the area of France now known as Brittany. This left the countryside of Britain relatively unpopulated and people from the German tribes of the Angles and the Saxons began to settle there. Beginning in the eighth century, Danish Vikings also settled in England, although it remained under Anglo-Saxon control.

Several important historical figures are mentioned in *Gytha's Message*. Here is a brief summary of these people:

King Edward: Edward was raised in Normandy in Northern France. In A.D. 1042, at the age of thirty-eight, Edward returned to England and was crowned king a year later. A very devout man, Edward built the famous Westminster Cathedral and collected many relics. In A.D. 1045 he married Edith of Wessex but they were childless and in A.D. 1066, Edward died, leaving no direct heir.

HISTORICAL NOTES

Harold Godwinson: Following the death of Edward, Earl Harold Godwinson, a distinguished military leader and the brother of Edith of Wessex, was crowned the last Anglo-Saxon King of England. Just seven months later, William the Conqueror invaded, and in the Battle of Hastings, Harold was killed and his army destroyed.

Edgar Ætheling: Before his death King Edward had appointed his grandnephew, Edgar, as king but due to Edgar's young age of fourteen, and the need for a military leader to defend England from William the Conqueror, Harold was crowned instead. Following Harold's death at the Battle of Hastings, Edgar was chosen as king but never crowned. Two months later he surrendered to William and gave up the throne. Although well-treated by William, Edgar made several attempts over the course of his life to regain the English throne, finally dying in Scotland around A.D. 1126.

William the Conqueror: Following the death of his father, Robert the Magnificent, William became Duke of Normandy at the age of seven. William claimed that he had a legitimate right to the throne of England and that several years before his death, King Edward, a cousin of Robert the Magnificent, had promised the kingdom to William. When Earl Harold was crowned king instead, William crossed the English Channel with an army of seven thousand men and invaded England. After defeating King Harold and Edgar Ætheling, William was crowned King of England, ruling until his death in A.D. 1087.

Aldred: As an influential bishop, Aldred assisted King Edward during his rule, including leading a failed military expedition against the Welsh. In A.D. 1058 Aldred went on a pilgrimage to Jerusalem, and in A.D. 1060 he was elected Archbishop of York, a position he held until his death in A.D. 1069. Upon the death of King Edward, Aldred crowned Harold king. When Harold was subsequently killed, Aldred supported Edgar and finally crowned William King of England.

Lanfranc: Another highly influential member of the clergy during the eleventh century, Lanfranc was born in Italy and then taught in France and Normandy before finally being appointed the Archbishop of Canterbury in England.

One of King Edward's greatest achievements was the building of the Church of St. Peter on an island in the Thames River. This became known as the West Minster or West Church which we know today as **Westminster Cathedral.** Completed just a week before his death, the cathedral has been the coronation site of all but four English or British monarchs, beginning with Harold and William the Conqueror.

HISTORICAL NOTES

Beginning with the early church, Christians began to preserve and revere the bodies of those who died for the faith. Over time these remains become more and more honored. These **relics**, as they were called, were believed to perform miracles and to impart God's blessing and protection to those who possessed them. Other relics included the clothing or other belongings of martyrs.

Sometime after the invasion, a beautiful tapestry called the **Bayeux Tapestry** was embroidered. Two hundred and thirty feet long by twenty inches wide, the tapestry depicts the events leading up to, and during, the Norman invasion. Today the tapestry is on display at a museum in the town of Bayeux in northern France.

IMPORTANT DATES

A.D.

911   King Charles of France invites Rollo, a Viking, to settle with his people in northern France where they adopted French customs, converted to Christianity and become known as the Normans

1043 Edward crowned King of England

1066 Death of King Edward and the Norman invasion of England

Timeline of 1066 A.D.

Jan. 5   Death of King Edward

Jan. 6   Earl Harold Godwinson crowned King of England

Sept. 28 William the Conqueror invades England

Oct. 14   The Battle of Hastings and death of Harold Godwinson

Oct. 15   Edgar Ætheling proclaimed King of England

Dec. 25   William the Conqueror crowned King of England

CONTENTS

ILLUSTRATIONS

Gytha's Message

Gytha's Message

Chapter I

The English Slaves

WEARY little crowd of wayfarers was approaching the town of Bristol, or Bricstowe, one bright spring morning in the year 1053. Most of them were tired, footsore, and ready to faint with hunger, and the boys and girls of the party would have lingered behind the rest had not their flagging footsteps been urged forward by the frequent crack of the driver's whip.

They were a party of slaves on their way to the famous Bricstowe slave-market—a motley crowd of men, women, and children collected from all parts of England. Fierce and savage many of the men looked, with their ragged unshorn sheep-skin garments and unkempt hair. The women and children looked even more forlorn in their helpless misery. Some appeared to be swine-herds and farm-servants of the meaner kind, while a few were evidently sailors and passengers who had escaped from the wrecks of vessels cast ashore during the winter gales.

Among the crowd, and apparently the weakest and most weary of them all, walked a boy and girl. Their feet were swollen and bleeding from their long walk over the rugged ill-kept roads, and several times they would have fallen to the ground but for the kindly help of a rough-looking sailor who walked by their side.

"Nay, nay, keep a good heart, my young sea-king; the wattled roofs of Bricstowe town are within sight, and—and then—"

"We shall be sold like cattle in the market," fiercely interrupted the boy.

"We will forget that, and think only of the good cheer the monks will bring us and the heal-ing lotions to cure our blistered feet."

"I want not their food, nor their medicaments either; I hate all monks," answered the boy, while his sister looked from her brother to their friend with a puzzled look in her white weary face.

"The saints hate all our race," she ventured to say at length, rather timidly.

"Then thy race, little maiden, must be bad in-deed or the saints harder-hearted than I have thought them, or they could not but have mercy

MEANER: *poorer, lowlier*
WATTLED ROOFS: *roofs built with woven poles supporting straw or other plant material*

on such as thee;" and he looked pityingly at the white worn face of the girl.

"Mercy!" repeated the boy scornfully; "our race asks not mercy at the hands of God or man —if there be a God," he added.

"Well, it is not our concern to ask too much about the business of priests and monks. I wonder what they will make of thee, boy," he added, with a faint attempt to laugh, as he glanced at the delicately reared lad.

"Set us both to tend swine, with an iron collar about our necks," answered the boy in the same tone of scornful defiance.

"Oh, Leofric, they will not put the slave's collar upon thee," said his sister with a burst of anguish. "We will tell them we are free-born, and English, like themselves, only shipwrecked as we returned from our long stay in Flanders."

"And did we not tell them this before, Gytha? I tell thee the saints and White Christ, as well as Thor and Odin, are revenging themselves upon us, the last of our race, for all that our fathers have done."

"Nay, nay, my young sea-king; I doubt me whether the old gods trouble themselves about such as we, whatever the saints may do," said his friend.

The boy's eyes flashed with angry scorn. "My fathers were mighty men, Vikings and Berserkers, and as great as the upstart Godwins of Wessex about whom we heard so much as we came through London." At this moment the miserable crowd was brought to a sudden standstill by a gay caval- cade sweeping through the gates of Bricstowe, and the slaves were huddled together at the side of the road to make room for the prancing steeds and ambling palfreys of the hunting party.

As they were passing near where Leofric and Gytha stood some mischance befell one of the hawks, and he slipped from his owner's wrist and would have fallen helpless under the horses' feet had not Leofric started forward and rescued him.

"Now that was right deftly done," said the gay young hunter as he received the bird from Leofric; and he would have slipped a piece of silver he had taken from his pouch into the boy's hand. But at the sight of the money Leofric started back with an angry flush upon his face that the hunter should think of paying him for the slight service.

Only two or three had noticed what had taken place, but the sailor seemed vexed that the money had been refused. "She needs it sorely enough," he said, as he looked at Gytha, "and since thou wilt not accept the aid of holy church and the good brethren, what wilt thou do for food now thou hast rejected this gift?"

"Take whatever is given me—the slave's por- tion," said Leofric, in proud defiance.

GAY: *light-hearted*
CAVALCADE: *a procession of riders on horses*
PALFREYS: *saddle horses other than war horses*

His friend laughed. "Thou wilt soon find what that is—nothing or rather less."

"Nay, but they will not let us starve; we are of some value as merchandise at least," said the boy.

"Such merchandise is left to the care of the monks, I tell thee; a meal more or less will not alter our market-value enough to make them feed this hungry troop, now that our journey is over."

Leofric groaned and would have grasped Gytha's hand, but at this moment she slipped from his side and fell to the ground just as they got inside the gates of the city. The driver thundered and cracked his whip in vain this time. Poor Gytha lay unconscious of it all and heedless of the driver or his threatenings. Leofric dragged the unconscious form of his sister to the shelter of a high wall, for fear she should be trampled to death.

He had scarcely laid her down when a gentle-looking woman, in the dress of a nun, stepped out of a narrow gateway close by. "Poor thing, poor thing," she said in a tone of tender pity, and raising Gytha's head she took a little bottle of cordial from a large pouch at her side, and poured a few drops down the girl's throat.

"She is very ill; I will have her carried inside and put to bed;" and without waiting for Leofric to speak, the nun hurried back to the little gate, and in a few moments Gytha was carried in, her

brother still standing in speechless, helpless bewilderment.

The kind sister noticed the dazed look in the
boy's face, and spoke a few words of comfort.
"I cannot stay to ask all I would fain know
about this girl, for each hour brings a fresh crowd
of slaves for the spring sales, each crowd more
miserable and hungry than the last."

"We too are slaves,—Gytha is my sister," said
Leofric in a subdued voice.

The nun looked surprised. "But it matters
not," she hastened to add, "the Church knoweth
no distinction between slave or free so they be
needy and she can help them; but I must away,
for others need my tendance I doubt not as sorely
as thy sister, and thou hadst better follow thy
master, or thou wilt be in worse case;" and the
nun hurried away on her errand of mercy, while
Leofric slowly limped after the crowd of slaves
that were still within sight.

Leofric might not have been allowed to linger
so long, but here in the narrow crowded streets
of the city, the slave-driver had all his work to
do to thread his way between the horses and lit-
ters and little groups of other slaves, while to
stand still and wait was almost out of the question; so he had to content himself with an occa-
sional backward glance, and when at last he saw
Leofric slowly limping after them, but without
his sister, he poured forth a volley of oaths.

FAIN: *gladly*

"Where is the girl?" he shouted as he at last joined the party.

"At the convent," sullenly spoke the boy.

The information was received with a storm of invectives. "Why can't the Church leave men to mind their own business? I would soon have roused her up with this;" and he cracked his whip as he spoke.

For the first time in his life Leofric felt thankful for the Church that could succour the helpless, down-trodden, ill-used slave and come between him and the lawless brutality of a cruel master. Gytha was safe for a little while at least, and he could not altogether repress a smile of triumph at the thought, while his master continued to curse the Church and all monks and nuns.

"The meddling hooded crows come feeding and pampering a herd of slaves, pitying them and preaching to them, until the lazy knaves believe they are as good as their masters. But I won't be cheated this time. I'll have the girl out of their old nest and in the market tomorrow or I'll pull the nest about their ears. Last year they robbed me of a woman—it was a clear robbery, I know, in spite of what the bishop said about the right of sanctuary; and they think to do the same again and take the girl that will fetch the highest price of the lot." So he continued to rail and grumble until the slave pen was reached, where they would all be huddled together until the next day.

INVECTIVES: *insulting or abusive language*
SUCCOUR: *give relief to someone in want or distress*
RAIL: *use harsh or abusive language*

Just as they reached this, the end of their journey, they were met by a monk and a couple of lay brothers bearing a basket of bread between them, which they at once began to distribute among the hungry crowd.

But this work of mercy was speedily stopped, for no sooner did the driver see what was going on than he kicked over the basket of bread and began to belabour the two younger brethren with his whip.

"Hold, hold!" shouted the monk; "lift not thy hand against the Lord's servants." But the man had worked himself into such a fury concerning his supposed wrong in the detention of Gytha at the convent, that, instead of desisting, he turned and struck the monk, dragging his cowl from his head, so that the few locks of gray hair were blown about by the wind. The sight of the hoary-headed monk thus assailed because he was doing a work of mercy and charity roused the anger of the bystanders; but before a blow could be struck the driver reeled and fell to the ground, while the blood poured from his nose and mouth.

The crowd of slaves and citizens started back in horror as the stricken man fell to the ground, and looked from one to another as they whispered, "The saints have cursed him for lifting his hand against the holy father."

No one ventured to go near him but the old monk, and he instantly stooped, and raising the

HOARY-HEADED: *gray- or white-haired*

man's head, loosened the blue tunic that was fastened about his throat, and then dispatched one of the younger brethren to the monastery for a famous potion, considered quite efficacious in such attacks in those days. But the crowd shook their head at the idea of a potion being given. "'Tis the curse of God and St. Peter, and naught will mend that, I trow," said one of the more outspoken of the bystanders.

"Doubtless he hath offended the saints," said the monk; "but he may desire to make restitution if he be but restored, and it is nathless our duty to do all we can to assist the saints in their work of mercy. Thou mayst give forth the bread, my brother," he said, turning to his other young helper, who was still rubbing himself where the whip had fallen hardest, leaving the citizens to pick up the bread and put it in the basket.

The lay brother cast a look of something like disgust at the swollen discoloured face of the prostrate driver. "Suppose he comes to himself again directly?" he said.

"He will desire that the hungry should be fed, my brother," quietly answered the monk; and he asked the crowd to stand aside and give the stricken man more air.

What the nature of his seizure was he did not say, but it was evident that he understood it; and the crowd were satisfied that if anyone could pene-

EFFICACIOUS: *effective*
TROW: *believe or think*
NATHLESS: *nevertheless*

trate into such a mystery Father Dunstan could do it, for he was the most skillful leech in Bricstowe as well as the most learned and holy monk in his monastery, so that the combined power this spiritual and physical knowledge gave him would certainly restore this slave-driver if anything could. But still the crowd was only half satisfied that the monk had interfered and stopped the saints in their work of vengeance.

Father Dunstan was too much absorbed in watching the stertorous breathing of his patient and the other symptoms that now began to develop themselves to pay much heed to the various whispers that were going on around him; and when at last the potion was brought he gave only a small quantity of it to the man, but once more sent back the messenger for help to the monastery that he might be carried thither without delay.

"Bid the brethren use all dispatch in sending needful bearers, and do thou go with all speed," commanded the old man. He seemed as anxious and interested in his patient as it was possible to be; and when at last four lay brethren came bearing a litter for the sick man he helped to raise him as tenderly as a nurse would raise a favourite child; and as he was borne towards the monastery he walked close at the side, still watching most anxiously every change in the breathing.

Meanwhile the bread had been distributed, and

LEECH: *physician or surgeon*
STERTOROUS: *with harsh snoring or gasping*

a pail of broth had followed to the slave-pen, all of which had quickly disappeared; and before their master had been carried away some of the slaves had sought a temporary forgetfulness of their misery in sleep. But Leofric was not of this number. He had taken his share of food with the rest, swallowing his pride at the sight of the bread, and now strengthened and refreshed he could think more calmly of what had befallen his sister and their master.

For once he was quite willing to believe in the power of God and rejoice in it, for He had justly punished their oppressor; but then came the puzzling mystery—if it was God's work to curse as He had cursed this man, how was it that the monks and the Church, who did their work in the name of God, tried to reverse it and take the curse away?

It was a puzzle—and think of it how he might and as long as he might, Leofric could not understand. At last he gave up the attempt and fell asleep, worn out with his long march, and for a time forgetting all his troubles and sorrows.

Chapter II

The Old Monk

EFORE the close of the next day Father Dunstan had two patients upon his hands; for Gytha's symptoms soon became so alarming that, although several of the sisters were well-skilled in the art of healing, none of their famous potions or decoctions seemed to relieve the poor girl, and so Father Dunstan was sent for to see her.

Perhaps, too, the sisters were all the more ready to send for the good father in the hope that they would thus hear something of what had really occurred near the slave-market, since the most contradictory reports had reached them concerning the matter, though they all agreed in this particular, that a wonderful miracle had been performed. What it actually was, however, no one knew exactly.

So Father Dunstan's visit to the convent was eagerly looked for by the curious sisters, and, having discovered that *their* patient was the slave of the stricken man, they become even more

DECOCTIONS: *extracts obtained by boiling down*

curious about the whole matter; especially since on being undressed Gytha exhibited marks of cruel violence about her delicate body. In telling this to Father Dunstan the sister accordingly spoke of her cruel master, and the reports that were in circulation through the town concerning his miraculous seizure.

But to her great disappointment the old monk shook his head. "The man is subject to such seizures, I doubt not," he said, "although this is greatly aggravated by the fury and passion he was in."

"Then thou dost not think that this is the work of God, to defend the honour of the Holy Church whom this evil man assailed in the person of her servants," said the nun, in a disappointed tone.

The old man rubbed his shaven crown in perplexity; "Nay, nay, I said not so, for we know that our God ordereth all things both in heaven and earth, and it may be He will turn this man's heart to Himself by means of this seeming vengeance."

"Then thou dost not think he will die," said the sister, who had already begun to build upon that contingency the hope of rescuing little Gytha from a life of slavery.

"Nay, God hath rewarded my poor skill in striving to snatch him from the hand of the destroyer," said the old monk, with something of exultation in his tone.

EXULTATION: *rejoicing, triumph*

The nun felt anything but gratified at the result. She had made up her mind that God would save Gytha by means of this man's death, and she could not altogether conceal her feelings. "That poor child will be shipped off to a Saracen slave-market and become worse than the paynim themselves. Is it worthwhile to save her now for such a fate?" she questioned rather angrily.

The poor old monk sighed. "I would to God I could save her and hundreds like her, who are sent into heathenesse from this our own Bricstowe market. Would that our saint king could know all the horrors of this slave-trade, then methinks he would deem it a good work to devote some of the money now spent in purchase of relics for the enrichment of churches, to putting an end to this evil traffic."

The nun stared at what seemed the monk's heretical words. "What work could be so good as purchasing relics that the hearts of the pious might be drawn by the contemplation of these to greater devotion?" she said.

"Works of mercy and deeds of charity," said the monk, somewhat shortly; "but now let me see the patient without delay."

The nun led the way to the infirmary, where Gytha lay still insensible on a little bed that had been drawn into a corner away from the other patients; for this convent-infirmary was rarely untenanted, especially at this season of the year,

SARACEN: *Arabian*
PAYNIM: *pagan, especially Muslim*
HEATHENESSE: *heathen nations*

when hundreds of over-driven slaves were arriving in the city almost every day.

Father Dunstan took as much pains and showed even more tenderness in examining this patient than he had shown her master; but this case, unlike the other, seemed to puzzle him greatly. "I cannot see that she is suffering from any disease," he said; "she is weak and worn out, but that would scarcely account for this death-like trance."

At the word "trance" the nun became more eager about her patient than ever, for to her it was almost synonymous with "miracle;" and in those days, instead of doubting the fact of miracles being performed, men were constantly on the look-out for the visible interposition of God on their behalf; so the sister may be forgiven for seeing another miracle, as she thought, in what this skillful monk said. After all it was only an exaggeration of the sweetest and divinest truth which we all believe, and which Christ Himself enunciated when He said, "Even the very hairs of your head are all numbered."

For nearly an hour did Father Dunstan sit and watch Gytha's faint, irregular breathing, and then, fearing his other patient might need him, or become restive under the restraint he had deemed it needful to impose, he left some directions about the medicines and drinks that were to be given her, and promising to come again in a few hours he went back to his other charge.

SYNONYMOUS: *the same as*
INTERPOSITION: *intervention*
RESTIVE: *restless*

To his great surprise the man had regained consciousness during his absence, and seemed much better. "I say, old man, that was an ugly blow you gave me," he said, as Father Dunstan went up to his bedside.

"Nay, nay, I gave thee no blow," said the monk mildly.

The man rubbed his eyes and passed his hand all over his head as if in search of some bandage. "Them hooded crows that were here just now wanted to tell me that the saint of this monastery or somebody like him had given me that knock down, and as they said you had been saving me, well I thought you must be the saint that knocked me over."

"Nay, nay, it was no mortal hand that struck thee down, my son," said the monk, in a solemn tone.

The patient shivered, and all the superstitious fears that he had been trying to reason down by the notion that it was the monk who had dealt the blow, returned upon him with tenfold force; for as he looked at the white-haired old man and noticed the thin emaciated frame and delicate hands, he knew it was impossible that he could have stricken him down any more than the young lay brothers could; and he trembled with guilty fear before this great supernatural power in the presence of which his brute strength had been but as the weakness of an infant.

He had offended the saints, that was certain;
and if this old monk had so far propitiated them
as to persuade them to restore him once more, he
would, of course, expect his reward—a gift to
his monastery, or some deed of charity, or some
concession made as to the future treatment of
his slaves. And whatever he promised he would
have to perform too; for he could never be beyond
the vigilance of this power that had struck him
down.

These were some of the thoughts that passed
through his mind while the old man stood watching him, and marveling at the improvement in
him. He, too, was indulging in some spiritual
visions concerning this man, in which he saw
him a true and faithful servant of God, rescued
from his evil life by the wonderful power that
had been exhibited in his cure.

But he was rudely awakened from these dreams
by his patient abruptly asking, "Well, old man,
what do you want to conclude the bargain?
There is a good deal of the vulture about you
hooded crows, all of you," and he tried to laugh.

"Speak not evil of God's servants, lest a worse
thing come upon thee," said the monk sternly;
and he turned away and left the room.

Again the man's guilty fears and superstitious
horror took possession of him. What a fool he
was to fight with, or offend, this supernatural
power that seemed to be against him, and that

PROPITIATED: *gained the favor of someone for someone else*

only the Church could understand or deal with; and then his thoughts went off in a business direction, and he wondered how many crowns he would have to part with to appease the offended saints. He was determined it should be a money bargain to be done at once, and got rid of; he would be hampered with no conditions as to the treatment of his slaves, or anything else; and then he began to wish Father Dunstan would come, both that he might conclude this business without delay and get away from the monastery.

But Father Dunstan did not come. Hour after hour passed, and the monk whose duty it was to watch by the sick, moved noiselessly about, and the faint sound of the monks' chanting the vesper service in the chapel, came to his ear, but Father Dunstan did not make his appearance, and again his superstitious fears were in the ascendant.

At length, after long watching and waiting, the door opened, and the old monk came slowly forward. "My son, I would that thou wert sleeping at this late hour," he said gently.

"Sleeping! who could sleep with—with," and there he stopped. "I want to know how many crowns the saints mean to make out of this—how much I am to pay to this monastery before I leave it."

"Thou mayst leave this monastery whensoever it pleaseth thee," said the monk, again moving away.

VESPER: *evening prayer*
IN THE ASCENDANT: *rising*

But the man stretched out his hand imploringly, "Stop, stop, holy father," he cried in alarm; "I will not call thee a hooded crow again, since the saints are offended at it; but stay one moment and hear me. How much am I to pay thee for curing me?"

"God Himself will repay me all I need. As I said, thou mayst depart—"

"Yes, but with this curse upon me," interrupted the man, again trembling with fright. "What can I do? what can I give to be rid of this, and go back to my business once more?"

The old monk sighed as he sat down and took the hard coarse hand within his delicate fingers.

"My son, God would have thee turn to Him for mercy and pardon for all thy past sins. He offers thee these without money and without price, because Christ died to redeem thee with His own blood."

The man stared, but in his gross ignorance he could not comprehend the divine message so simply delivered. "I know nothing about this clerkly learning. I never saw a book in my life; talk to me of crowns and the market value of a slave, and I am as good as any in Bricstowe. Come, shrive me of this curse, and tell me what I must pay for the whole business."

The old monk sighed. "God would have thee to practice mercy rather than give of thy silver even for the enrichment of His church, and it is

GROSS: *extreme*
CLERKLY LEARNING: *reading and writing*
SHRIVE: *free*

of this I would fain talk to thee in the morning."

"Thou canst talk now; but I warn thee, holy father, I will not have any of thy meddling with my slaves."

"God Himself hath—but I forgot; the rules of this house must be obeyed," and instead of bestowing the customary blessing as he turned to depart, the old monk held up his hands and said, "God be more merciful to thee than thou art to thyself," and immediately left the room.

He went to his patient early the next morning, for he too was anxious to conclude a little business with him, and one in which he felt deeply interested now. Gytha was still very ill, but she would probably recover after some rest and care, although her recovery could not in any case be very rapid. All this was explained by Father Dunstan, who added, that the girl certainly could not be sold just yet, for no one would buy her except one customer, and he would pay a small sum for her, and take the risk of her recovery, provided her brother was sold with her at a moderate price too.

"They are the most valuable slaves I have got," grumbled the man, "and worth double the sum that is offered for them."

"The girl is not worth a silver penny to thee now, but may be a great expense before thou canst sell her in the regular way. But it was not in this way I meant to talk with thee on this matter. Hast thou no thought, no thankfulness, for the mercy that hath been shown to thee?"

"I tell thee, holy father, I will give a goodly sum to thy monastery if thou wilt lift this curse from me," said the man, somewhat impatiently.

"And I tell thee that neither God nor Holy Church can accept thy money except it be given with deeds of mercy and charity. God loveth mercy more than money, and I ask thee in His name to show mercy to this boy and girl, or—"

"Nay, nay, hold; curse me not again, holy father," interrupted the man in an agony of fright; "thou shalt have the boy and girl to sell at thy own price, only give me thy blessing, and let me depart without further mischance."

The old monk smiled at the man's ignorant, credulous fears, but it was the only way by which he could hope to benefit Gytha and her brother; nay, it was the only way in which the Church could often protect the helpless and defenseless from the lawless violence of such men; and who could cast blame upon them for securing this advantage in an age when men acknowledged little law but their own will, and no power but brute force, except what the Church exercised over them occasionally?

So Father Dunstan took care, before his patient departed, to have all the necessary forms required for the transfer of Leofric and his sister to their

CREDULOUS: *overly willing to believe or trust*

new master duly completed, and the boy handed over to the care of the brotherhood. Then, with sundry cautions regarding his health, and the potions to be taken during the next few days, he bestowed the customary blessing of the Church, and the man departed, grumbling inwardly at the loss of two such valuable slaves, and determined to make up their price in his subsequent sale of the rest.

Father Dunstan hastened to the convent to tell the nuns of his success, and that they would not have to give up Gytha yet; and even when she did leave the convent it would not be for some faraway Saracen slave-market, but only to become bower-maiden to some lady in Wessex.

"But she cannot travel even so far as that," said the sister in some dismay.

"She needeth not to travel yet; her brother will doubtless journey thither in a few days, but she is to abide here in thy care until some trusty messenger or pilgrim can be found who will bear her to the household of her new master; for he is young and something of a Viking, I take it, and careth not to be burdened with maiden folk."

"Then wherefore hath he bought her?" asked the nun, who had taken a great liking to Gytha, and still hoped she might become one of their sisterhood.

"She is to be bower-maiden to his sister," answered Father Dunstan; and then, noticing the

BOWER: *a lady's private apartment in a medieval hall or castle*
BOWER-MAIDEN: *a lady's maid*

sister's disappointment, he said, "Nay, nay, grieve not, my daughter; God hath work to be done in the world as well as in the convent, and sometimes I question whether the world would not be better if fewer departed from it to shut themselves up in peace away from its storms and turmoils."

This was a speech the nun could not at all understand; but Father Dunstan often said queer things, such as no one else thought of; but she did not forget the saying, although she was soon absorbed in her various duties of tending the sick and overlooking the management of the household.

Chapter III

At the Convent

EOFRIC'S new master was no other than the young man whose hawk he had rescued as he was entering Bric-stowe. Passing the slave-pen where the lad and his companions were confined, he recognized the proud boy who had so angrily refused his gift, and immediately stopped and spoke to him.

"Well, my young Berserker, art thou as ready to fight me now as when we last met?" he asked, with a merry laugh.

"I am always ready to fight any man when he insults me," said Leofric.

"Well, 'tis evident the slave's collar will never bend thy proud neck, though it may break it very soon. 'Tis a pity a young blood like that should be lost," he added, turning to his companion, and putting his hand to his pouch, as if to count the number of crowns it contained.

"What! wouldst thou buy the boastful young

swash-buckler?" asked his friend, noticing the action.

Leofric noticed it too, and pushing his way closer to the stockade that surrounded the pen, he said in an earnest tone: "If thou hast a mother, or sister, who needs a gentle bower-maiden, spend thy crowns on my sister, and, for the love of God, save her from a Saracen slave-market. I can fight my way through the world; but Gytha—" and at the mention of his sister and the probable fate that awaited her, a groan of heartfelt anguish burst from the poor boy's lips.

"Come, come away, we can do nothing to help him, and there are hundreds here in the same evil case. I hate to come near these slave-pens;" and the two friends moved away, leaving Leofric alone in his misery.

But they had not gone far before the first suddenly turned back again. "How many crowns does thy master ask for thee and thy sister?" he asked.

Leofric shook his head; "I know not; and my master, as thou callest him, is at the monastery being cured of the blow the saints gave him in their wrath yesterday."

"Come, Gurth, thou surely art not in earnest about buying this boy. Who is to be master between you?" added his friend, who had again joined him.

"Oh, we will both be masters," laughed Gurth,

who was as willful in his way as Leofric himself; and without another word he turned in the direction of the monastery, where at once he saw Father Dunstan and soon made known his errand.

The kind-hearted monk was quite ready to enter into the plan of rescuing Gytha, and undertook to have her included at a very little additional expense in the bargain that was to be made for Leofric, and likewise to keep her at the convent free of all charges until she should be well enough to travel, and undertake the duties of a bower-maiden.

Truth to tell, Gurth was not nearly so anxious about Gytha as he was to have Leofric for a personal attendant, and but for the old monk removing all difficulties out of the way the poor girl might have been left to her fate. It would be a shame, he thought, to reduce such a fine spirit as the brother's to the usual condition of a slave, for he admired the very qualities that had hitherto proved a hindrance to Leofric's gaining the favour of those with whom he had been lately associated, and he intended to make him rather a companion than a slave.

So when the bargain was concluded, and Leofric was handed over, Gurth's first care was to provide him with more suitable garments, but without the usual badge of slavery—the iron collar round the neck. He also allowed him to go with bare throat, showing the blue figures that had been punctured there, and of which he was so proud. It was thus with no small pleasure that Leofric went to the convent a few days afterwards to see Gytha before departing for their new home.

The little girl had been informed of something that had taken place, for she was better now, and could sit up a little while each day, but she was not at all prepared to see her brother look so changed, not only in his garments, but in his whole manner and countenance. She did not notice at first the proud exultation with which he held up his head, and showed his bare throat, for she was so overjoyed to see him smile once more that she forgot everything else.

"They have told thee all about our new master, my sister," he said, taking Gytha's thin white hand in his. "I would go to the end of the earth with Gurth, my master, and—"

"And thou dost call this man master without cursing him," uttered Gytha, in astonishment.

"Yes, Gytha, I am proud to serve such a master. See, there is no outward badge of slavery—no ring about my neck bearing my master's name upon it; and as he told me yester-morn, if I tried to run away from him I should certainly succeed, for no man would know I was a slave; but, Gytha, he hath bound me to him more fast than with rings of iron about my neck, for he hath taken captive my heart, and my feet would forget their work if I tried to forsake him. And he hath bought thee too, my sister, although he will not claim thee at this time. Thou art to be bower-maiden to his sister, who hath been long sick, and needeth gentle tendance. Art thou not glad, Gytha?"

"Yes, I am, if thou art; thou knowest I am always pleased with what pleaseth thee;" but, even as she spoke, the little girl heaved a deep sigh.

"Nay, nay, thou must not be sad, little one," said her brother.

"But—but thou art going away from me, and what shall I do without thee?"

Leofric, too, looked troubled as he tried to soothe his little sister, but at length he said, "Thou dost not know the duties of a bower-maiden, Gytha; thinkest thou the nuns would teach thee?"

"I know not whether they can teach me that, but I am learning 'Our Father,' and 'The Creed.'"

But this information did not seem to please Leofric; "I would thou hadst left clerkly learning alone; thou knowest that none of our race had ever aught to do with the Church."

"Nay, but the Church rescued me when I was dying," said Gytha, "and the good sisters here would be sorely grieved if I refused to learn what they are pleased to teach me."

OUR FATHER: *the Lord's Prayer*
THE CREED: *the Apostle's Creed; an early formal statement of Christian beliefs*

"But thou sayest they cannot teach thee aught but the knowledge pertaining to the Church or the convent, and what will that profit thee?"

Gytha shook her head; "I have not thought of the profit, my brother, but how I might pleasure the good sisters who have been so kind to me. Think, Leofric, I should have died but for their care."

"Yes, they have been kind, I trow; but look you, Gytha, thou art a slave, and thy master and mistress would fain have thee skilled in the duties of a bower-maiden and not learned in clerkly arts; for they, as we, are not over fond of the Church, saith my master."

"And what, pray you, are the duties of a bower-maiden? Did thy master tell thee?"

"Now, Gytha, is it likely that those whose business it is to learn the use of the cross-bow, and the training of hawks and falcons, should know aught about the dyeing and mixing of herbs, or when the floors should be strewn with fresh rushes?" said Leofric loftily.

"Well, I will ask the nuns if they can tell me aught about the herbs or rushes," said Gytha; "but I must learn also what they will fain teach me," she added.

"Oh, thou canst learn all they please; but it were better for thee to forget it as soon as thou leavest the convent, for clerkly learning is of no use in the world, as thou knowest."

"Then dost thou think God hath nought to do with the world?" asked Gytha simply.

"What can He have to do with it?" asked Leofric. "If there is a God, as the monks say, then He is wiser than the saints, more powerful than Thor, or Odin, and kinder than any holy sister in this convent. Now think you, if there was such an One, He would suffer men to make slaves of their fellows, or let them imbrute themselves with drunkenness as all our countrymen seem to do?"

"The Normans and men of Flanders are not thus swinish," said Gytha.

"No, and it were well if Englishmen could learn something of Norman abstinence and Flemish handicraft."

"Leofric, I know something of this," said Gytha, "and it may be that my knowledge of the Flemish embroidery will please my mistress better than if I were learned in the use of herbs."

"But thou hadst better learn the uses of these too, and leave all convent-learning alone, for that is only fit for nuns, not for bower-maidens."

Leofric could not stay long with his sister, for they were to depart early the next morning on their journey, and there was some furbishing of arms and cleaning of horses to be attended to.

Poor Gytha was very brave, and resolutely kept back her tears as long as her brother was

IMBRUTE: *degrade*
ABSTINENCE: *self-control*
FURBISHING: *polishing*

with her; but as soon as she was left alone she broke down utterly. "Oh, Leofric, Leofric," she sobbed, "come back to me. I cannot live without thee."

"Hush, hush, little one," said one of the nuns; "thou must not grieve so sorely; thou wilt see thy brother again soon. The Church hath saved thee from the bitter pangs that many suffer who never see friends or kindred after their parting in the slave-market."

"I know, I know," sobbed Gytha passionately; "but oh, why is not the God you talk about as kind as the Church?"

The nun started at the bold, strange question. "God is kind," she said at length; "the Church doth but try to show the love of God to the world that lieth in wickedness."

"But why doth the world lie in wickedness? why are there any slaves if God is kind, and yet more powerful than the old Norse gods?" said Gytha; for this question of her brother's had troubled her.

But the sister could only shake her head in shocked surprise. "I know that 'God is love,'"[1] she said, "and that is enough for me."

"Yes, because thou art in a convent away from the tumult and violence of the world, but—but what is there for people who live in the world?"

The gentle-hearted nun could only shake her head. "The world is an evil place, full of violence

[1] I JOHN 4:8

and cruelty, and 'tis best to fly from it to the shelter the Church hath provided," she said.

"But all cannot fly from it; some must abide outside the convent howsoever cruel the world may be; what hath the Church for these?" asked Gytha.

But before the nun could answer Father Dunstan stepped forward. He had entered the room unnoticed, and heard the girl's last troubled question.

"So thou dost want to know how thou art to live in the world, since the convent cannot shelter thee very long?"

Gytha coloured and look confused. She would not have dared to ask such questions of the holy Father Dunstan, as she had of the young nun. But the gentle smile on his face and the kindly pressure of his hand reassured her, and she ventured to say:

"The Church hath provided a shelter for the weak and defenseless, but what can those do who cannot fly from the world?"

"Abide in the love of God, little one."

"The love of God?" repeated Gytha.

"Yes, my daughter, the love of God reaches beyond the convent and beyond the Church—even to the world that is full of violence and cruelty."

The young nun was scarcely less astonished than Gytha, and she said, "Doth God love violence and cruelty, then?"

"Nay, I said not so, my daughter, but He loveth the world, while he hateth the evil that is in it. He loveth the men and women in it, though he hateth the evil they commit."

"But—but if He is great as well as kind, why doth He not stop the evil?" Gytha ventured to ask.

But the question seemed to puzzle even wise Father Dunstan—or at least how to answer in a way that Gytha might understand. At length he said: "Hast thou ever been into the convent-school, where there is often a great din of learning tasks and repeating the paternoster? Well, as thou knowest, the sisters love quiet and would fain have it, but the young knaves who come to learn must needs make a din with their learning; and so the good sisters have patience and bear it for the sake of the paternosters being always re-membered. And so, I take it, God dealeth with the world. It is His great school, and He hath given to the Church the work of teaching these His noisy scholars what He, their Father, would have them do."

"And God loves the people who are in the world?" exclaimed Gytha.

"Yes, my daughter, more tenderly than a mother loves her baby, only more wisely and patiently. Thou dost teach in the school, my daughter," he said, turning to the young nun.

"Yes, holy father," she answered meekly.

PATERNOSTER: *literally "Our Father" in Latin, another name for the Lord's Prayer*

"And dost thou not love some of thy little scholars?"

"I cannot help loving some of the little winsome knaves," she replied, as if fearing a rebuke.

"And do these never trouble thee with their frowardness and willfulness?"

"Oh, yes, some whom I love best seem the most willful," said the nun.

"Thou dost not love the willfulness, but thou lovest the little knaves in spite of it—hoping to conquer and subdue that by and by. Is it not so?"

"Yes, that is it—I do want to see some of my little scholars holy monks and nuns," exclaimed the sister earnestly.

"And just so doth God hope, and wait, and work, noting the violence, and evil, and sins that are in the world, but bearing with them because He loves the sinner, and hopes to see him some day not a monk or nun—God doth not want all men and women to become monks and nuns,— but He doth desire that all men should believe in His love—the love He hath showed in the gift of His Son Jesus Christ, whom He hath sent to take away the sin of the world."

"How did He take it away?—how could He?" asked Gytha, who had listened with breathless attention to every word that fell from the old monk's lips.

"Only in one way, my daughter,—by dying for

FROWARDNESS: *continual disobedience*

it—giving up His life a sacrifice because men had sinned themselves away from God and could not come back because their sins had piled up a great mountain between them and God. The blood of Christ could alone remove this, and make the way plain and easy for men to go to God; and now it is so easy that when once a man feels and knows he is a sinner, he has but to turn to the Lord Christ and ask Him to pardon all the evil of his life, believing that He can and will pardon him and make him fit to be not merely a monk or nun, but holy and fit to dwell with Christ and the saints in heaven."

"And we can believe this and turn to God, without coming to live in a convent all our life?"

"Yes, little one, though many do come. It would be better for the world, I think, if a few were to abide in it."

"I must abide in it," said Gytha, with something of a sigh.

"Nay, grieve not, my daughter, that God hath called thee to abide in the world; for He can give thee work to do there as well as in the convent—work thou couldst not do, perhaps, if thou wert to abide here."

Chapter IV

The New Home

PRING glided into summer, and summer had waned into autumn, before anyone suitable as an escort for Gytha had been found journeying towards her new home. But the time had not passed unimproved, for Gytha was anxious to please her mistress, and had diligently learned all that the sisters could teach her concerning the various uses of herbs and the proper preparation of rushes for the floors. In weaving and embroidery she was already very skillful, and had begun to learn the clerkly art of reading and writing, that she might, by and by, be able to copy and illuminate a psalter or missal for Leofric.

She would have been well-contented to spend all her days, or at least some years of her life, in the convent, busying herself in helping the sisters, and learning from them the lessons of wisdom and gentle patient forbearance.

But Father Dunstan met with a party of pil-

ILLUMINATE: *to decorate with gold, silver or brilliant colors*
PSALTER: *a book containing a collection of psalms*
MISSAL: *a book containing prayers*

grims at last, who were willing that the girl should travel in their company, and who promised to deliver her safely to her owner's care; and with these Gytha was obliged to depart, deeply sorry to leave the convent, but looking forward with joyful anticipation to seeing Leofric again.

After a weary journey of nearly a week—for they stopped at every shrine and holy place to offer prayers on their way—they at length reached the end of their journey, and Gytha was ushered into a large hall—the best room of the house, where an elderly lady and gentleman sat talking and watching the movements of a favourite hawk which was strutting up and down among the rushes on the floor, and blinking at the fire that had been newly made in the center of the room. There was no chimney, and the rafters above were blackened with the smoke that curled and wreathed itself among them before finally passing out of the hole just above the fire. But this did not seem to inconvenience either of the occupants of the room, and Gytha had stood at the entrance some minutes before she was noticed.

At length the old thane raising his head from watching the hawk, saw Gytha standing near the door.

"What wouldst thou, child? from whence art thou come?" asked the thane quickly.

"I am from the convent at Bricstowe, where I

THANE: *a freeman who owes service to an Anglo-Saxon lord, especially military service* have stayed ever—ever since I became thy slave," said Gytha in a lower tone.

"Wife, dost thou know aught of this?" asked the old man, turning towards his wife with a puzzled look.

But before she could answer, Gytha had caught sight of Leofric in the outer hall, and forgetting all else but that her brother stood before her, she uttered a faint scream and rushed into his arms.

The lady stepped to the door to see the cause of Gytha's sudden agitation.

"Do you know this girl?" she said rather sharply to Leofric.

"She is my sister, whom my master Gurth bought to be bower-maiden to the Lady Hilda."

With a gesture of dissatisfaction the lady turned away to inform her lord of this addition to the household, while Leofric drew Gytha aside to say a few words to her alone.

"Thou art grown tall and strong, my sister," he said, with something of admiration in his tone, as he noticed the improvement in her whole appearance.

"Yes, the sisters have taken good care of me," said Gytha smiling through her tears.

"In truth they have, and I hope they have taught thee somewhat of the things I spoke of, for thy mistress is not likely to pass over lightly any lack of knowledge in these things."

"Yes, I have learned the use of the herbs, and

how to prepare rushes, as well as some other things," answered Gytha.

"There must be no clerkly learning brought here," interrupted Leofric quickly; "no one believes in the Church in this house; at least there is no favour to it, and some hate it right sorely."

"That is thy master Gurth, I trow; but, my brother, thou wilt not hate holy Church now thou hast seen what it hath done for me."

"If it did naught but succour the oppressed and feed the hungry, I could say no word against it, but I have heard things from my master concerning his kinsman, Earl Harold, son of Godwin, the great earl who died some months since, that have made many men say they will have naught to do with such a Church."

"I know not what I should do, or the world would do without it," said Gytha. "My brother, the world would be as a den of wolves and evil beasts, where the weak would soon be devoured or trampled down, and then the strong would fall upon each other. Nay, nay, Leofric, the world could not last long without the Church."

"Nor yet without a woman's tongue, it seemeth," said her brother laughing. "Why, Gytha, who taught thee to use thine so freely? I never heard such a long speech from thee before."

Gytha blushed. "I cannot be silent when the Church is spoken against," she said.

"Then I fear thou wilt soon get into sore

trouble with thy mistress. Little sister, I tell thee, thou must be careful; for thine is no easy task. None can please the Lady Hilda, they say. But I am forgetting mine errand. I am going with my master to take his ban-dogs to try their strength on the great bear. Some of the serving maids will take thee to thy mistress;" and with an affectionate embrace he hurried away just as the lady again appeared at the door.

"Come here, child, and tell me who brought thee hither, and what thou canst do."

"An it please thee, noble dame, a band of pious pilgrims brought me hither, and I can spin and work deftly with the needle, and the nuns have taught me much concerning herbs and roots."

"'Tis well they can teach something useful," said the lady, with something of a grunt. "Come, child, I will take thee to thy mistress;" and the lady led the way through various passages and halls to a room at the other end of the house.

This, like the first, was supplied with a fire burning in the center; and Gytha was at once impressed with the wealth and importance of the family, that they had two rooms in the house fitted with holes so that a fire could be made in them.

In this, however, there was more evidence of wealth and luxury than Gytha had ever seen gathered into one room before. The walls were hung with rich tapestry, and the floor strewn thickly with clean rushes; whilst ranged against

BAN-DOGS: *dogs that must be kept tied because of their ferocity* the wall were several carved oak chests, and on a table drinking horns tipped with silver, and a branched candlestick made entirely of that precious metal.

Gytha had time to notice all this, and also that there were several young girls spinning in the further corner; for the lady left her near the door while she went forward to speak to the invalid who was sick, and inform her of her arrival.

"How art thou today, Hilda?" asked the lady gently.

"How should I be, but full of pain this cold day?" answered the invalid ungraciously

"Didst thou know Gurth had bought a serving-maid for thee when he was at Bricstowe last spring?" asked her mother.

"He told me of some such folly, but I paid little heed to his words. Is it true, then?" she asked.

"Yes; the girl hath just arrived, and I have brought her at once to thee. Come hither, child," she said, turning towards the door.

The invalid eyed Gytha critically as she came forward. "She is not quite so clumsy as a muzzled bear," she said; "and as Gurth has bought her I must keep her, I suppose."

"If she is useful to thee thou canst do so; if not, she can be sold again," said the elder lady quietly.

"Where is Gurth, that he hath not been to see me today?" asked the invalid, in a peevish, fretful tone.

"Well, a great bear hath been caught somewhere beyond the Watling Street, and brought hither; and of course Gurth hath gone with the house-carles to take the ban-dogs to try their strength upon it. I had some ado to keep thy father within doors when Gurth came talking about the bear, and I must return to him, or he will even now follow the house-carles."

"Do not tarry with me," said Hilda impatiently; and she took no further notice of Gytha until the door closed upon her mother. Then beckoning her closer to her couch, she said, "Come, child, and tell me thy name, and what thou didst learn at the convent."

Remembering Leofric's warning, Gytha answered slowly, "I learned the duties of a bower-maiden as well as the holy sisters could teach me."

"And they could not teach thee how the heart-ache could be cured, I ween, though they can doubtless cure the pains and rheums of the body?"

Gytha looked with pity on the fair pain-drawn face of her mistress, and wished she could hear some of the sweet comforting words she had heard from Father Dunstan's lips, but she was afraid to speak after Leofric's warning. Her mis-

HOUSE-CARLES: *household men-servants who also per-formed military service for their lord*
WEEN: *suppose or imagine*

GYTHA BEFORE HER NEW MISTRESS

tress was little more than a girl, she could see, and yet the lines in her face told a tale of long years of suffering not too patiently borne, and the restless anxious look in her eyes and hovering round her lips told of a longing unsatisfied, of a hunger and thirst never appeased.

She turned uneasily on her narrow couch, which, though it could boast of being elegantly carved, was only supplied with pillows stuffed with straw, so that it was little wonder the lady's limbs often ached, or that she longed to be able to walk about as others did.

"So thou knowest the duties of a bower-maiden," said Hilda, after a pause. "Canst thou be patient under rebuke that is perhaps undeserved?" she asked.

"I will strive to please *thee*," said Gytha. "The nuns have taught me by example as well as by their words that I should at all times be patient."

"Thou shalt tell me more another time of what thou didst learn from the nuns. Canst thou spin and embroider? Go, look at what my maidens are weaving yonder, and tell me if thou canst do such work as that."

Gytha crossed over to where the shuttles were flying so deftly between the fingers that plied them, and looked at the linen cloth they were weaving.

"I do not think I could work so quickly, but

the sisters said I kept web and woof of the straightest."

"Thou wilt soon learn to use the spindle quickly if thou hast learned to use it well;" and the lady relapsed into silence and apparently forgot all about Gytha, and that she was standing near. Gytha waited without a word or sound to disturb her mistress, and nothing broke the silence but the rattling of the shuttles and the crackling of the burning logs on the hearth.

At length the lady roused herself from her reverie, and then seemed surprised that Gytha was standing near.

"What art thou waiting for?" she asked in a sharp tone.

"Thou didst not bid me go," said Gytha.

"Few wait for that; they are all too glad to get away from me, as thou wilt be, I doubt not, ere long;" and the invalid sighed as she again turned on her unyielding pillows. "Thou mayst go," she said carelessly, and Gytha moved towards the recess where the girls were spinning.

But every head was bent more closely over the work, and the spindles flew in and out faster than ever, as Gytha drew near. She was hungry and tired, for she had walked some miles that day, and when she noticed the averted looks of those who were to be her companions she felt so disheartened that she could scarcely restrain her tears as she stood silently near them.

WEB AND WOOF: *the interlacing threads in woven cloth*
REVERIE: *being lost in thought*

Her mistress at length looked up, and seeing Gytha still standing, she said, "Rowena, take the girl to the cook and get her something to eat."

Rowena laid aside her work and beckoned to Gytha to follow; but she took care to keep at a distance, and when they had left the room this precaution became even more apparent.

The kitchen was at some distance from Hilda's room, for the house had been added to from time to time—each addition, whether a simple lean-to or large hall, having always been on one side; so that the original kitchen still remained where it had at first been placed, occupying one end of the house, while Hilda's apartments were the latest addition at the other. It was thus through a labyrinth of passages that Rowena now led Gytha; and although some of them were quite dark she never slackened speed, or held out a hand to guide the stranger through the gloom. On entering the kitchen she said in a loud voice.

"My mistress bade me bring this slave-girl for something to eat."

The cooks and scullions, who were all very busy preparing supper, turned and looked at Gytha.

"Slave-girl!" repeated the chief cook. "How long is it since thy father was a slave, Rowena?"

"My father is a franklin, and owns his six hides of land, and 'tis a shame to bring slaves

FRANKLIN: *a medieval English landowner of free but not noble birth*
HIDE: *a measure of land area, usually 120 acres*

and make bower-maidens of them beside franklins' daughters;" and Rowena tossed her head in
haughty scorn.

"What are we to give her?" asked one of the
scullions, who evidently enjoyed Rowena's vexation.

"Anything will do—any odd bits that have not
yet been given to the swine," answered Rowena.

"Did thy mistress bid thee say that?" asked
the chief cook, making a dash at Rowena with
the huge spit she had in her hand.

But Rowena dodged aside and avoided the
blow, and then with a derisive laugh ran away,
leaving Gytha in this new crowd of strangers.

"Come, child, and eat this slice of cold boar's
head, while I draw thee a horn of ale; that will
serve thee till supper, I trow," said one of the
cooks, as she pointed to a block of wood for
Gytha to sit down.

But the poor girl's heart was too full for her
to eat. She thought of the homely but pleasant
repasts at the convent, and instead of eating the
meat she burst into an hysterical flood of tears.

"What ails thee, child? Is not the food good
enough for thee?" said the cook rather sharply;
for she could not understand hungry people crying with food in their lap, and what more could
people want, especially slaves, than plenty to eat
and drink? so she repeated her question with a
shake, as Gytha did not answer.

REPASTS: *meals*

"I can tell thee thy master and mistress have eaten worse food than that," she said.

"Yes, yes, it is very good—better than I often had at the convent," sobbed the girl.

This seemed to appease the angry cook a little, and she said, "Well, I am glad it is not the food that displeaseth thee; as for that froward wench, Rowena, thou must not heed aught she says. Come, eat up the meat, and thou shalt have a horn of strong ale."

"I cannot eat," sobbed Gytha, trying to keep back her tears.

"Nay, nay, but thou must, child, for thou wilt have enough to do with thy mistress and these saucy wenches of bower-maidens. Thine will be the hardest place in the house, I trow, so drink up the ale—it will give thee a little heart for thy work; and when thou hast nothing to do thou mayst come to the kitchen, though it is not all bower-maidens I will have about me."

"Thank you," said Gytha, thankful for these few words of kindness; and seeing her new friend would be offended if she did not try to eat what had been given her, she swallowed a few mouthfuls; but she only sipped the strong ale, for she had not been used to such drink as this.

Chapter V

Hilda

YTHA did not return to her mistress' room until after supper; for, fatigued with her long walk and the excitement that had followed, she fell asleep in the kitchen, and did not awaken until supper was being served.

Hilda's bower-maidens did not take their meals in the great hall with the family and men-servants, but in an adjoining room with the upper serving-maids of the family; and here the distinction of rank was as strictly observed as at the master's table. Rowena and her companions sat near the head of the table, but Gytha, as a slave, was seated near the foot; while at the same time there were open comments made upon her position and presumption in aspiring to be a bower-maiden on an equality with the daughters of franklins or free-men.

Hilda rarely left her rooms, but had her meals served before the maids left her, when one was left in attendance while the rest came to the

servants' hall. When supper was over Gytha and
her three companions returned to the other end
of the house, and at once commenced their evening duties. Two stout rails were slipped under
the legs of the couch on which their mistress lay,
and each of the four girls taking one end, she was
carried into an adjoining apartment—her bed-
chamber. While one prepared the bed, and
another held her night-linen to air before a
brazier, the other two undressed their mistress;
but no one would accept the assistance of Gytha.
When she silently volunteered to perform some
little service about the room she was rudely
pushed aside, or the things snatched out of her
hand, while her mistress seemed totally unmindful
of her presence.

The next day it was the same. No one seemed
to want Gytha, or her services; no work was given
her to do, and she spent the greater part of the
day in looking out of the little lattice window,
or watching the flying spindles of her companions.

But her solitary musings by the little window
were not altogether without fruit. The middle
of the day being fine and warm, the window had
been opened, and, taught by her good friends the
nuns to be always on the look-out for some herb
or root that could be turned into useful account,
she looked carefully down into the herb garden
to see what was growing there, and then to the

BRAZIER: *a metal pan filled with hot coals*

meadows beyond to see what they would afford. There was not much beyond grass and a few fine old trees, but round the roots of these she thought she descried some moss, which, when dried, made most excellent pillows—far softer than straw she knew, for she had lain upon one while she was ill, and had helped to dry the moss, and make others afterwards. So she resolved to gather some of this, and if she could get it dried in the kitchen, she would make her mistress a more comfortable pillow than any she now possessed. Perhaps Leofric would be able to help her in gathering the moss, and she resolved to see him, if possible, before he went with his master into the great hall to supper.

Her mind being occupied with her plans for doing this work the time passed more rapidly, until she was able to leave her mistress and go in search of her brother.

"Oh, Leofric, I want some of that moss grow-ing under the trees there; can you help me to pick it?"

Leofric shrugged his shoulders. "What do you want with moss?" he said.

"To make a pillow for my mistress. Oh, Leo-fric, she does look so ill, and so unhappy. I wish I could do something for her."

"Nobody can do anything to please her; but I'll get the moss for you, if you want it."

"Yes, I do want it. Can you go now while

DESCRIED: *caught sight of*

your master is with my mistress? I can go for a little while."

Leofric was by no means so eager to get the moss as his sister. Looking after his master's hawks and dogs was much more to his taste; but still, with Gytha for a companion, he was not unwilling to help. They picked nearly all they could find in this spot, and Gytha sent her brother to look for more that they might gather another day, while she carried what she had to the kitchen, to ask the cook if she might dry it there.

"Yes, yes, you may bring it here, if you don't put it in my way; and I'll lend you an iron dish to keep it in."

This was all Gytha wanted, and she was soon busy picking it over and placing it in the dish, as she had often done before, and then it was laid near one of the fires where it was not likely to be in anybody's way.

The next day passed in much the same way, only a larger quantity of moss was gathered, and Gytha was scolded for being so long absent from her mistress' room.

But another difficulty had presented itself to her mind now, and one in which neither Leofric nor her friend the cook would be able to help her. She had got the moss to stuff the pillow, but how was she to get the linen cloth to make the case? Leofric rubbed his forehead ruefully as she mentioned this difficulty to him.

At length he said, "Couldn't some of the other bower-maidens give you this?"

"I daresay they could, but—but I should not like to ask them," she said. She had been careful not to let her brother know of her uncomfortable position with her companions, for fear of rousing his anger against them. "Couldn't your master give you a piece of cloth such as I want?" she said, after another silence.

"I don't know, I'll ask him, if you like; but I must tell him what you want it for."

To this Gytha readily agreed, and the next day Leofric brought the cloth to make the pillow-case, and a request from his master that he should see the pillow when it was made.

"Oh, yes," answered Gytha, "and if he will give it to my mistress I shall be so glad." And so, when the pillow was finished it was carried to Gurth, with a request that he would present it to his sister.

"Yes, that will I right gladly," he said, as he took the soft yielding cushion in his hands; and he left his occupation of training the falcons, and went at once to his sister's room.

"See here, my lady sister, how deftly thy new bower-maiden hath been at work for thee!"

"What is it?" asked Hilda, rather languidly.

"A pillow of moss upon which thou mayst lay thine head without fear of its aching."

"I would it were a pillow for my heart then,"

LANGUIDLY: *without interest*

said the lady with a deep-drawn sigh; but she deigned to take the pillow in her hands, and express her approval of it. Then her brother gently raised her head, and removing the straw-pillow, replaced it with the one he had brought.

"Now, Hilda, rest thine head on that, and tell me all that troubles thee."

"Nay, nay, thou hast heard all my troubles before today, and canst answer none of my questions, and as I believe not now in any God, since they have all failed to help me, there is little more to be said."

"But why should it trouble thee so much Hilda? what difference can it make to thee whether there is a God or not?"

"Not much now, perhaps; but dost thou not remember the songs our nurse used to sing to us —the songs of Valhalla? Now, if there are no gods, then there can be no Valhalla, and what was I made for?"

It was a question that had often puzzled Gurth himself, but one to which he could find no answer. But at length he said, "I would not let this thought trouble me; think of something else—of the stores of linen thou hast in thy chests, of anything but this, since thy question cannot find answer."

"It were easy for thee, Gurth, to put such a question far away, if even it came into thy mind; for thy life is happy and busy and useful—but mine, what is it? Why am I made to suffer here,

VALHALLA: *Viking "heaven," literally "hall of the slain"— the hall of Odin in Norse mythology where warriors who died in battle were received* when there is no Valhalla to compensate me beyond? why am I the mockery of gods and men?"

"Nay, nay, my sister, speak not so bitterly. No one mocks thee; but many pity and would fain help thee."

"And I hate to be pitied; I despise pity," exclaimed Hilda passionately. "I want to take my place in the world, and go to the hunting-parties and bear-baitings, and instead of that, I must always lie here, a helpless, miserable creature."

Truly she was miserable, and her brother knew it; and though he would have given all he possessed to lighten her affliction and make her less unhappy, nothing he could do seemed likely to effect this. With a sober, saddened countenance he at length took his leave, and soon after the lady's supper was served, and then Gytha and three of her companions purposed to leave. But, to everyone's astonishment, Gytha was commanded to remain with her mistress today.

It was the first service she had been allowed to perform as yet, and she felt rather nervous at being left alone with the exacting lady; and when the others left she sat in the furthest corner of the room scarcely daring to breathe.

But the heavy tapestry curtain had no sooner fallen over the doorway than the lady called Gytha to the side of her couch. "Now, child, tell me why you made this pillow; I did not bid you do it." She spoke sharply, and poor Gytha feared she was very angry, and so it was with trembling apprehension that she said, "An it please you, noble lady, I thought the straw was hard oftentimes when thy head ached."

"And that was thine only reason?" asked Hilda, in a more gentle tone.

"An it would give thee some ease I could not have a better reason," said Gytha.

"Then thou wouldst fain ease my pain if thou couldst! Well, since thou canst not do that, thou shalt amuse me with what thou and the nuns did pass the time in at the convent."

Gytha felt afraid lest she should offend her mistress again as she went on with her recital, and remembering Leofric's warning she kept carefully to the account of the sisters' works of charity. But the lady soon stopped her with an impatient exclamation. "Didst thou never hear of a God in the convent? or is He one so dreadful that they were afraid to tell a child like thee?"

"Oh! no, indeed; for God loves me, although He is so great and high and holy!"

"*Loves* thee, child?" exclaimed her mistress.

"Yes, Father Dunstan told me so very often; and he took me into the convent library once, and read the very words where it said so in God's own word—the Saxon Scriptures I think he called it."

"I wish I could see this Father Dunstan, or this Book—the Saxon Scriptures," said the lady with a deep-drawn sigh.

"Father Dunstan is the most learned and pious monk in Bricstowe," said Gytha, losing something of her fear in the joy she felt at being able to talk about this teacher whom she so deeply reverenced and loved.

"I have never spoken to a monk or a nun in my life; no one would ever allow me to do it; but I have often felt curious about them, so thou must tell me everything thou canst remember about this Father Dunstan, and what he taught thee, unless thou hast forgotten it all."

Gytha shook her head. "Nay, I could never forget Father Dunstan, for he taught me that there is a God for me—a God who loved me although I was only a slave, and could never hope to be a nun and leave the world to serve Him."

"Then thou wouldst like to be a nun, Gytha?" said the lady.

"The world is full of violence and cruelty, and the convent seems the only place where rest can be found for those who are not among the strong," said Gytha, as if in excuse of the longing that had come over her again since she had been in this strange household.

"Yes, I suppose the convents do afford a refuge for those who cannot take care of themselves— a rest as you call it," said the lady musingly.

"But Father Dunstan says that God did not send us into the world to rest, but to work, and that He would rather have me at work for Him in the world than praying and singing in the convent, or He would have made it plain and easy for me to stay there, instead of sending me here!"

"Nay, nay, child; God could not have sent thee here. If He is a God at all He must know that none in this house, or of our race, have ever bowed to any but the old Norse gods, that are well-nigh forgotten, except by a few like my father and my grandam," said the lady quickly; and yet she looked as though she wished Gytha would contradict this statement.

Poor Gytha hardly knew what to say; but at length, encouraged by that strange, gentle, yet pleading look in her mistress' face, she said, "Father Dunstan was very learned and very wise, and the holiest monk in Bricstowe, and he said God sent me here, and—and—"

"And what, child?" said her mistress impatiently; "speak out; don't be afraid."

"Leofric said I must never speak about God in this house," said Gytha, trembling.

"But what did Father Dunstan say? tell me that."

"He—he said, God was sending me here to bring a message to somebody—to somebody perhaps that needed it as much as I did; and I have thought that some of the scullions in the kitchen, who are slaves as poor as I am, might be glad to hear it some day."

"And what is the message?" asked the lady eagerly.

"That God loves all men; that He so loved the world—all the men and women in it—that He gave His only Son to die that they might be redeemed from their sin and their selfishness, and know and love Him and be happy forever. It is just the right kind of message for slaves," added Gytha, "and I want to tell some of them about it when I see them unhappy, only—"

"Is it only for slaves?" asked the lady eagerly.

"Nay, Father Dunstan said it was for all men, and was the greatest joy of his own life; and he was not a slave, for I heard the sisters talking one day, and they said he was of noble birth and very rich, until he became a monk, and gave all his wealth to the monastery."

"Then he is almost a saint instead of a slave," said the lady.

"Yes, the sisters often said so; and he heard it one day and seemed sore grieved thereat, and he told us then that it was only because of God's free love to all men, and because Christ died to cleanse him from his sins, that he dared to hope he should be saved." Gytha had forgotten her fear by this time, and spoke so earnestly and so warmly, and her mistress had been listening so intently to every word that fell from her little bower-maiden's lips, that neither had noticed the return of the other attendants, until a slight noise

among the rushes as one of them tripped in crossing the floor announced the fact.

"Thou shalt tell me more tomorrow about this
wonderful message," said the lady, as she once
more settled herself on her new pillow. "Thou
mayst go to thy supper now, child;" and Gytha,
wondering not a little at all that had happened
during the last hour, hurried from the room.

Chapter VI

Leorfric and His Master

LTHOUGH Leofric and Gytha were attached to the same household they did not see much of each other, for Leofric was always in close attendance upon his master, joining in all his frolics, innocent and otherwise, and sharing in all his secrets. If there was a bear-baiting with the ban-dogs, or a trial of skill among the king's archers and the citizens of London, or a meeting of the Witan at Westminster, at which Earl Harold was expected to speak words of wisdom or counsel for the good of the nation—wherever or whatever it might be, if Gurth were there his faithful follower was with him, or not far away. In the Witan Gurth could stand with the free burghers of London and the thane landowners by right of his birth; but Leofric stood some distance below, among the ceorls, but watching closely the face of his master he knew when to lead the popular applause at this, the lower, but

WITAN: *an Anglo-Saxon council made up of nobles, church officials and other officials, to advise the king*

by no means less powerful half of the great national council.

Leofric's "Yea! yea!" was generally followed by a hearty response from his companions, and usually coincided with the wishes of the burghers and thanes—the Commons of this early parliament; and thus the ceorls, although not privileged to vote on any of the questions brought forward, became the public opinion, which the council could not wholly disregard; for the "Nay! nay!" of the ceorls, usually given in accordance with the opinion of the thanes and burgesses, if passed over without notice, might serve to give rise to a riot within the city.

It would have been as well, perhaps, for Gurth and Leofric if the Witan had sat more frequently than it did; for they would at least have been kept out of a good deal of mischief that was not always quite harmless.

It was not often that the household heard of these wild escapades of its young master; but Leofric came to Gytha in great distress one day.

"What hast thou been saying to the Lady Hilda, that she should favour these miserable starveling monks even more than her own brother?" he demanded angrily.

"Nay, I knew not that she did favour them," protested Gytha.

"Such a thing was never known in this house

BURGHERS: *inhabitants of a borough or town*
CEORLS: *freemen of the lowest rank in Anglo-Saxon England, peasants*

before, and thou must have been the cause of the mischief."

"Nay, what have I done? My mistress hath often questioned me of late concerning Father Dunstan and my manner of life in the convent, but she hath said nought to show that she hath favour towards all monks."

"But she hath, and thou art the cause, and a fine trouble is like to come of it," grumbled Leofric.

"Why, what hath thy master done?" asked Gytha curiously.

"Nought but a joke was intended, and none but an old shaven crow would have made so much ado about the loss of a few silver pennies," said Leofric.

"Oh, my brother, thou hast not committed the sin of robbing a holy father?" uttered Gytha in horror.

"Robbed him! I tell thee it was but a joke, though perchance a sorry one for him, if those few poor pennies we took from his pouch were all he had been able to collect for his monastery that day;" and Leofric burst into a loud laugh.

But Gytha did not look upon it as a laughing matter, for the tears were in her eyes as she said, "Oh, Leofric, if the vengeance of the saints should fall upon thee as sorely as it did upon that cruel man who took us to Bricstowe, and as it hath upon—;" and Gytha stopped suddenly, shivering with apprehension.

"Upon whom else hath these vengeful saints spent their vengeance?" asked Leofric.

"Nay, nay, speak not against the saints," implored Gytha; "thou knowest they are not vengeful, but merciful, or they would not have aided Father Dunstan in healing that evil man, our master."

"Well, I will not call them vengeful. But who else have they smitten down?" asked Leofric curiously.

Gytha drew a step nearer to her brother. "I have heard it said that it is because none in this house honour Holy Church, or are obedient to her laws, that my mistress doth suffer so sorely." The words were spoken in a whisper, and Gytha looked round cautiously as she uttered them.

Leofric did not start or look surprised, for he had heard the same thing, but he said, "What dost thou think about it, Gytha?"

But she only shook her head. "I am not learned or wise," she said.

"But thou art learned in all the Church teacheth. What did Father Dunstan say about such matters?"

"He ever taught that God is merciful and loveth all men, desiring that they may love and believe in Him, and be happy forever."

"Yes, Father Dunstan said something like that to me; but I have heard this that thou hast told me about the Lady Hilda, and I say with my

master, 'Is it fair that a gentle lady should be so
sorely stricken for the evil that others have
done?' Is thy God more just than men thus to
afflict the weak and let the strong go unpun-
ished?"

Poor Gytha did not know what to answer, but
she looked very much distressed as she said, "I
know that God loves all men, for He loves me;
but I can't understand many things that happen in the world, and Father Dunstan said I
never should—there would always be something
to puzzle people,—but if I kept fast hold of this
truth that 'God is love,' and waited patiently to
see the end, I should understand a good many
things that I could not learn in any other way."

Leofric, however, was growing tired of his
sister's quiet talk. "I would there were no meddling monks," he exclaimed, "for my master is
summoned before Earl Harold's hall-mote to
answer for these charges, and though the earl
hath little favour towards monks, Gurth feareth
they will gain his ear in this."

"Nay, nay, not if the charge be an unjust one,"
said Gytha; "for even I have heard that the
great earl loveth justice before all things."

"But the monks will have their way, justice
or no justice, and doubtless they will bring other
charges against my master." Leofric did not say
what these other charges were likely to be; but
Gytha soon heard from others in the household.

HALL-MOTE: *a gathering at a manor house for a court*

For some cause, or because it suited his humour just now, Gurth had not been content with quietly ignoring the Church and its laws, as his father did, or merely railing against priests, monks, and bishops, but had waylaid a party of pilgrims, bound them with thongs with their faces towards their palfreys' tails and old clouts fastened to their clothes, and in this ignominious guise had driven the horses some miles out of the right road.

His next escapade was to fire the hayricks of a neighbouring convent, and frighten all the nuns; and now he laid wait for a friar returning from gathering the Church dues, and emptied his pouch, after beating him with a stout cudgel and rolling him in the mud.

Many of the household thought, as did their master, that these were good jokes, and rather to be commended than blamed, for in that age little was thought of such violent deeds unless they were committed against the rich and powerful, who were able to take reprisals. But to Gytha the offenses were serious crimes, not so much on account of their violence as that they were committed against Holy Church; and she wept and prayed over them in secret, and made herself so miserable before the day of trial came for the culprits that her mistress noticed her distressed looks.

"What aileth thee, child? Thou hast looked

CLOUTS: *rags of cloth or leather*
IGNOMINIOUS: *humiliating, disgraceful*
REPRISALS: *use of force to pay back for damage suffered*

sad and woe-stricken both yesterday and today,"
said the lady in a voice of unusual tenderness.

For answer Gytha burst into tears, and for a
minute or two nothing was heard but her convul-
sive sobs, for her companions instantly stopped
their spinning in their wonder at Gytha thus
daring to obtrude her griefs upon her mistress'
notice.

"Heed well, weave well," said the lady reprov-
ingly as the pleasant hum of the spindles was
stopped, and the girls bent their heads over their
work again, while their mistress beckoned Gytha
to come close to her couch.

"Is it for thy brother thou art grieving,
child?" she asked gently.

Gytha bowed her head. "He, too, is summoned to appear at the hall-mote to be holden
tomorrow," she said.

"To answer, with Gurth, my brother, for
robbing a holy friar of some silver pennies," said
the lady, calmly repeating the charge.

Gytha's tears flowed afresh as she heard it.
"Nay, but child, tell me why thou art so sorely
grieving for this?" said the lady. "Is it because
thou fearest the punishment for them, because
Earl Harold is just, and will not lightly pass over
the evil doings of even a kinsman and his follower? I tell thee, child, I am glad it hath reached
the great earl's ears, and if I could see him before
the hall-mote were holden tomorrow I would say

OBTRUDE: *intrude*

to him, 'Give them such a punishment that they will feel it and remember it to the end of their life.'"

Gytha forgot her grief in the astonishment she felt at hearing her mistress speak like this, for she loved her brother most dearly she knew. "Most truly do they deserve punishment for so grievous a sin against Holy Church," she said slowly and sadly.

"Nay, but I was thinking more of them than of their sin against the monk. I love my brother right dearly, and would fain see him such a man as Earl Harold himself; but this can never be unless he be brought to think of other things than he doth at present, and so I trust our earl may compass this by the punishment he shall award them for their evil doings, for Leofric is a right noble knave as well as Gurth; but they need discipline and some stern lesson they are not likely to forget. And now, Gytha, put away thy tears, and try to be glad, as I am, that their evil deeds have been brought to light. The monk they robbed was not such an one as thy Father Dunstan, I ween," she added with a smile.

Gytha was puzzled—more puzzled than ever; but she could not but believe what her mistress had said, for she knew that she loved her brother most devotedly. Thinking of this brought to her mind something she had heard her good friend Father Dunstan say one day, that God did not

COMPASS: *accomplish*

punish or afflict men out of revenge or merely to punish them, but that they might be made better, which was just what her mistress was wishing for Gurth; and then came the thought, was it because God loved this lady that he had afflicted her?

When the rest of the bower-maidens had gone to supper Gytha was as usual called to the side of her mistress' couch, for it had come to be an established rule now that this hour should be devoted to conversation between mistress and maid.

"Thou dost think me very harsh and cruel, I ween, in what I said awhile since; but think not I have no pity for the light-minded knaves. I will help them to bear their punishment if I can do it without harm to them; so think not that I am without love for them."

"Nay, I know thou dost love thy brother, even as I love Leofric, only thine is—is a better love than mine—more like God's love for us," said Gytha, half-choking with tears again.

"God's love for us like my love for Gurth!" exclaimed the lady; "nay, nay, thou dost not know the tender love there is between us. This evil that he hath committed against the monk is done for love of me, I ween, although he told me not of it. Hast thou not heard it said that God hath stricken me with this sore sickness because our race hath ever rebelled against Him and the laws of Holy Church?"

"I have heard it said," answered Gytha; "but

may it not be that God hath afflicted thee, as
Earl Harold will punish Leofric and his master,
that thou mayst be the better for it?"

The lady started, and Gytha felt half-frightened at the boldness of her speech; but she
hastened to add, "If God loves us He must want
us to love Him and become better, and Father
Dunstan said this was the reason why He often
sent people trouble and affliction."

The lady lay with clasped hands looking at her
little maid. "Child, child, if I could believe
that," she said, "it would ease my pain as nought
can ease it now. But no, no, the news is too good
to be true for me; our race hath always hated
and despised thy God, and I must bear the punishment;" and she covered her face with her hands
and groaned in the agony of her soul.

Poor Gytha was scarcely less overcome, and
forgetting the difference in rank for once, she put
her arms about the lady's neck, and sobbed out,
"Oh no, no, God does love thee, dear lady;
Father Dunstan said the message was for everybody who would listen to it and believe in it.
Thou hast listened ofttimes of late, and thou will
listen again."

"Listen! Yes, Gytha, Gytha, though I cannot
believe what thou dost tell me, I am never so
peaceful as when listening to thee and thy stories
of God's love; but I cannot believe—no, I cannot
believe it will reach to me."

"But, dear lady, it hath reached me, and I know now that God loved me a long while before I knew it or cared about listening to it, and I, too, came of a race which hath hated and despised Him, and Leofric now glories in this."

"Even as his master doth, I ween. But can it be that any race hath been so evil as ours?" questioned the lady.

Gytha hastened to repeat several stories she had heard from Leofric illustrating the hatred of his forefathers to the White Christ and the Church.

"But thou, child, thou hast ever a gentle soul, while I—I am proud and hard and selfish, caring for nothing but my own easement."

"I, too, was proud, even when I had nought to be proud of. Nay, I gloried, as did Leofric, in coming of a race that were Vikings and sea-thieves and cared not for any God."

"But thou wert never so evil as I am, Gytha. Leave me now, child. I would fain think of what thou hast told me, and if I can believe in thy God I will, and if not—Leave me, leave me now," she abruptly added; and with a silent prayer to God for her unhappy mistress Gytha left the room.

Chapter VII

The Sentence

 ARL HAROLD sat in the great hall of his house in Wessex, and about him were gathered his thanes and ceorls, and a mixed company beside, for all who had complaints to make against any within his earldom were free to bring their cause before him. Among the complainants today stood two or three monks, while with the culprits appeared our two friends Gurth and Leofric. The former seemed inclined to treat the whole matter still as a joke, but Leofric looked sullen, and scowled fiercely at the monks whenever they looked towards them. He was angry for his master's sake, and because his oath was of so little value in this primitive court of justice that the word of six like himself would only be of equal value with the monk's, so that whatever excuse might be urged in extenuation of their offense the monk might very easily deprive them of it, as he was the only witness.

But when at length it came to their turn to

EXTENUATION: *an attempt to partially excuse an offense*

step forward and face that grave noble man, whom all England trusted, as well as those gathered round him, the monk did not seem at all inclined to make the worst of the case; indeed the holy father closed his speech with a word or two about the rashness of youth in extenuation of their offenses.

But Earl Harold was by no means disposed to take a lenient view of the matter. He had expected better things of Gurth Godrithson, the prop of his father's house, and soon to hold thane's rank. For his slave, Leofric, there was excuse, because he was a slave, but for his master there was none.

In a grave, saddened voice the earl descanted on the enormity of his offenses, their cowardice, and cruelty. He did not say one word about upholding the honour of the Church; but, what touched his hearers far more deeply, he spoke of the insult offered to God, who had a special care for the poor and friendless.

He then imposed a heavy fine upon Gurth, and condemned Leofric to three days' solitary confinement in a barn.

Gurth went home thoroughly humbled and spirit-broken. The amount of the fine was nothing to him, but he feared he had forfeited the earl's good opinion forever. "He expected better things of me." He repeated the words again and again to himself, as he sat alone with

DESCANTED: *talked at considerable length*

his hawk and hound, alike unconscious of their quarreling or caressing him. He did not care to go to Hilda's room, for she would want to know all that had happened, and would probably ridicule the earl's words.

So he sat alone during the rest of the day, pondering and wondering what Earl Harold had expected of him, since it seemed to him there was nothing else in the world for him to do. The next day he wandered out into the fields and woods, after seeing his father about the cattle that would have to be delivered today—the fine that he was condemned to pay. He felt lonely and sad, and missed Leofric very much, for there was no one else to condole with and pity him for his misfortune, as he chose to consider it.

The next day Leofric returned, bearing an urgent message, or rather command, from the earl, for Gurth to go to him at once. Such a command from his lord, Gurth dared not disobey, but it was with slow and reluctant steps that he turned towards the house of the Earl of Wessex, while Leofric turned towards the woods to ponder over his disgrace, as his master had done.

But his return had not entirely escaped observation, and Gytha, hearing of it, had immediately obtained leave from her mistress to go and see her brother; and so before he had passed beyond the stockade that surrounded the house Gytha's hand was laid upon his shoulder. Leofric shook

CONDOLE: *express sympathetic sorrow*

it off almost fiercely. "Leave me to myself," he said; "I don't want even you, Gytha."

"Oh, Leofric, don't you be angry with me too," said the girl, the tears welling up to her eyes as she spoke. "My mistress is sore fretted that her brother hath not been to see her these three days, and so no one can please her."

"My noble master is hurt, I doubt not, at the great earl's words to him; but what hath his punishment been to mine?" said Leofric bitterly.

"Were you beaten?" asked Gytha in a trembling whisper, as she gently laid her hand upon his shoulder again.

But Leofric shook his head. "I was not worth even that, and there lies the bitter sting. I am a slave, and though my master may trust me as a free-born follower, nought but slave's work is expected from me by others. If the earl had said to me what he did to my master, Gurth, I would rise like a man, and throw away these witless plays; but I am a slave, not deemed worthy of punishment like other men, and nought but witless work expected of me."

Gytha tried to comfort her brother, but her words were all in vain at present. It was useless and hopeless for him ever to think of doing better; and in this mood he left her, and wandered off to the woods to indulge his bitter thoughts alone.

Gytha did not go back to her mistress at once, but went to one of the outhouses, where she could give vent to her grief unseen; for an undefined fear that Leofric would run away had suddenly taken possession of her mind. What if he should do this, and she should never hear of him again? never hear whether he died of cold in the woods, or made good his escape to the far-off Flanders, where they had lived so long. That was where he would go, she thought; and then she prayed that the vessel bearing him thither might not be wrecked, as the one was that brought them to England. This peril over, there was little fear that Leofric would be made a slave again. He had often told her that he could escape from his master at any time, and no one would know he was a fugitive slave, and the exulting words he had so often uttered about this time came back to her mind so very vividly, that the fear soon grew into a certainty, and she felt sure she should never see her brother again; and then her grief broke out afresh.

How long she sat curled up on the pile of straw where she had thrown herself she did not know, but she began to feel stiff and cold at last, and when she crept out of her hiding-place she saw that the shadows of evening were darkening the sky, and the stars beginning to peep out one by one. She hurried back to her mistress' apartments, half-frightened that she had been away so long. But before she got there she was met by her companions, who had all been sent away.

"You are not wanted any more than the rest of us," said one; "Gurth is with our mistress—hath deigned to pay her a visit at last—and 'tis hoped he may please her now he hath come, for 'tis ill work trying to please her now."

Gytha did not wish her companions to see her in tears, and so, with a murmured word of thanks, she turned back and went out into the yard to lean on the stockade to watch for any sign of Leofric coming back. Perhaps he might come to speak to her once more, or to get some extra article of clothing, and she stood waiting and watching for more than an hour; but no footfall sounded along the wood path or broke the silence except the moaning of the wind between the leafless branches of the trees.

At last she turned towards the house, where lights were gleaming between the chinks of the shutters, and the sound of laughing and scolding could alike be heard.

Supper was smoking on the table when Gytha entered—a huge boar's head, flanked by joints of beef and pork, which the servants brought in on spits straight from the kitchen fire. Gytha hardly knew whether to sit down at the table with her companions, or go to her mistress at once; but at length she decided to go, for supper in the great hall was being served, and Gurth would be compelled to leave his sister.

She found her mistress alone, as she expected,

and Hilda at once called her to the side of her couch.

"Why, child, what is the matter?" asked the lady in surprise, for Gytha was shivering with cold, and at her mistress' question she burst into tears.

"Nay, nay, no more tears, Gytha, for 'tis as I hoped it would be; the earl hath not sought to crush the witless knaves, though his punishment seemed severe, but he hath sought to bring them to a better mind, and 'twas for this Leofric was kept from his master these three days."

But Gytha's tears could not be stayed. "Leofric hath told me he cannot do better, for no one expects aught of him but slave's work," she sobbed.

"Nay, but the earl hath spoken of him to his master, and Gurth hath promised for him that he shall no more rob poor pilgrims, or fire nuns' hayricks, but learn some useful handicraft, or to be more skillful in the use of the bow and arrows."

But to the lady's surprise, Gytha's tears only flowed the more freely, when she heard this. "Oh, my brother, my brother!" she wailed; and kneeling down by her mistress' couch, she told her all her fears concerning Leofric.

Hilda looked deeply concerned. "It may be as thou sayest, but I hope he will yet come back, for Gurth will lose a trusty and a noble servant,

STAYED: *held back*

I trow, and will not be so earnest in his efforts to amend his own ways."

"I fear, I greatly fear, he will not come back," sobbed poor Gytha.

"Thou hast been watching for him at the stockade, I trow, until thou art cold to thy bones. Hast thou had supper?"

"Not yet; I am not hungry," said Gytha.

"But thou needest a posset to warm thee. Fetch me yonder flagon, child; it hath some wine grown in our own vineyard; and bring me the drinking-horn, with a little water and honey, and thou shalt set it in the wood ashes on the hearth, and it will soon warm thee. There now, if the witless knaves would set themselves to learn how the growth of the grapes could be improved, it would be well; for 'tis said that all the old vine-yards are declining, both in the quality of the grapes and the quantity they yield; and if they be not improved shortly, England will have to send across seas for her wine, as she now doth for her fashions."

"Nay, but the vineyards look to be flourishing," said Gytha.

"They are not what they were. 'Tis said the Romans planted them when they made the great roads that run straight through the land, and goodly wine in plenty did they yield them, but 'tis little we get from them now."

The lady watched the colour as it slowly came

POSSET: *a hot drink of sweetened and spiced milk curdled with ale or wine* back to Gytha's pale face as she drank the warm posset, and when she was more calm, and somewhat revived, she said, "Come now, child, tell me why thou fearest thy brother hath run away."

Gytha told her all she could remember of the conversation with Leofric.

"So the knave is sorely grieved because he hath not been punished!" said the lady. "What dost thou think of that, Gytha?"

Gytha shook her head. The whole affair was a puzzle to her, and her mistress all at once seemed to be lost in thought. At length she said, "Dost thou remember what thou didst tell me about thy God afflicting and troubling those whom He loved, and whom He would fain have to love Him?"

"Yes; Father Dunstan said it was God's way to trouble those most whom He loved best."

"Then if that be true, and God dealeth with us as we deal with each other, then—then—oh, Gytha, thy God hath a little care for me, though I come of a race who have ever hated Him."

"Nay, it is not a little care, but a great love, that God beareth towards thee, and if thou wilt only believe this," and Gytha clasped her hands and looked imploringly into her mistress' face.

"I will try. I will go into a convent where I can learn all I want to know, and thou shalt come with me, Gytha, to tend me when I am sick, and help me to learn all the sisters can teach us."

It seemed that this was not the first time Hilda had thought of going into a convent, but it was the first time she had ventured to speak of it to anyone; and now, after she had talked of it a few minutes to Gytha, she begged her to keep it a secret for the present. "I must talk to Gurth first, and then to my mother and father, before I can do this thing;" and Gytha wondered what Leofric would say if he should hear she had retired to a convent to spend the rest of her days.

But these reflections were speedily interrupted by the return of the rest of the bower-maidens, and then her mistress insisted that she should go and have supper too, after once more warning her to keep silence upon what they had been talking of.

But this and everything else went out of Gytha's head a few minutes afterwards, for on her way through the passages to the other end of the house she met Leofric, who had just come in quite tired out with his long walk.

Gytha uttered a faint scream of joy, and threw her arms about his neck. "Oh, Leofric, I am so glad, I am so glad," she said.

"So glad—what about?" asked Leofric in surprise, for he wanted his supper now.

"I thought—I thought you had run away," hesitated his sister.

"Gytha, Gytha, couldst thou think me so low, so ignoble, as to think I should leave my master because I am left free as himself to come and go as I will without slave-badge or token? Nay, nay, my sister, did I not tell thee aforetime that Gurth had left me without chains or collar about my neck, but that he had made my heart fast to his own—had bound me with a chain more strong than any forged by smith's art?" He spoke in a grieved, passionate tone, and Gytha hung down her head, utterly abashed at the suspicions she had entertained against him.

"My brother, I am very sorry," she faltered.

But Leofric scarcely noticed his sister's words. "Hast thou told thy mistress of these thy base thoughts concerning me?" he demanded in the same angry tone.

"I—I was afraid—"

"Then ask the Lady Hilda to let me speak to her," he interrupted; and Gytha felt compelled to yield to his request and ask her mistress to see him.

The lady smiled when she heard Leofric's indignant denial of his sister's suspicions.

"I were base indeed not to feel bound to such a master as mine," he said in conclusion.

"Thou art a true and trusty knave, I see," said the lady with a smile, "and if thou and thy master would only think of doing some honest work when you are not hunting and hawking,

IGNOBLE: *dishonorable*
ABASHED: *ashamed*
BASE: *low*

my father and Earl Harold would have less to complain of concerning thy wild doings. Couldst thou not see to the vineyards and fields? they are greatly neglected, I trow."

"I will do aught that my master bids me," said Leofric promptly.

"I will talk to him about the matter. Thou art a true and trusty knave," concluded the lady admiringly, as Leofric turned to leave the room.

Chapter VIII

A Mad Act

ILDA thought it would be easy to turn her brother's attention to the improvement of the land, especially to the vineyards, which but a short time back were famous for the quality and quantity of grapes yielded; but in this she was disappointed. Gurth would study nought but the use of spear and lance, sword and battle-axe, or the art of shooting with the long and cross bow.

"Then thou wouldst learn to play at war," said Hilda, only half-pleased at her brother's choice of employment.

"Nay, nay; our earl doth counsel that all true Englishmen shall learn the use of these weapons, for though the Normans were driven out of London but a short time since, England hath not seen the last of them he feareth; and the Danes are restless and the Welsh dissatisfied."

Hilda laughed. "Then there be wars enough to prepare for, I trow; and so it becometh helpless maidens, who can neither fight nor run, to look for shelter that foes dare not invade."

"What dost thou mean?" asked Gurth, for he could detect a seriousness underneath the apparent lightness of his sister's tone.

"What shelter is there but such as the Church affords for helpless ones like me?" and the lady sighed.

"Thou dost not surely mean the convent! Hilda, Hilda, I tell thee, if thou dost shut thyself up there I shall give up all my newborn hopes of being useful—of being my country's man, that Earl Harold hath inspired."

"Nay, but hear me, Gurth. Thou hast often heard me talk of the restless longing I had to know something of what the Church teacheth; and from what my new bower-maiden Gytha had told me, I think it can give me what neither thou nor my mother, nor all my heaped-up treasures can give—peace and rest to my troubled, restless heart."

Gurth left his sister's couch, and paced up and down the room with hasty strides. "Hilda, Hilda, I cannot spare thee for the convent," he said at last. "Thou knowest not the power thy quiet room hath over me. Promise me this, my sister, that until the time comes, until the need arise, thou wilt not seek to leave thy home."

Hilda yielded a reluctant consent at last, but she sighed deeply as she gave the required promise, for she thought she could never have the many questions of her heart answered—the deep longing of her soul satisfied—unless she could retire to a convent and learn all the sisters could teach her of their holy faith.

Gytha, too, was disappointed, although, for Leofric's sake, she was glad to remain where she was, since he was much opposed to her going into a convent. Like Gurth he was to learn all the arts of war and all the discipline of a soldier, that they might in due time be enrolled among the earl's bodyguard, which was their highest ambition, and deemed reward enough for all the toil and fatigue they might have to undergo.

So while Gurth and Leofric practiced with the long-bow and spear, or lance and battle-axe, Hilda and Gytha were scarcely less industrious at home—Gytha with her spindle, and her mistress in directing the work of her maidens. Since they could not go to a convent they were determined to be useful at home, and what work could be more noble than preparing for the time —which they hoped might never come—when England would require their dear ones to go forth and use in real earnest the weapons they were now learning to handle?

So the spindles flew faster than ever, and the embroidery-needle was used more deftly; for two great chests were to be filled with linen and embroidery to be sent to Flanders in exchange for two shirts of mail, so closely woven of links of steel that no arrow should pierce them, though battle-axe might shiver breast-plate and corselet.

When the shirts of mail were bought, more linen was woven for the purchase of whole suits of armour; and Gytha shared in the work and the joy of presenting them to their destined owners, and in seeing her brother hardly less gaily dressed than his master.

So the months and years glided on, with little to disturb the peaceful lives of either Hilda or Gytha, until Gurth went in the train of Earl Harold to visit the Duke of Normandy, and brought back the vague report that Duke William aspired to mount the throne of England when their saint-king Edward died.

Hilda looked concerned, but Gurth only laughed at her fears. "Fear not, fair sister; no Norman duke will rule in Westminster while Harold lives. I tell thee, he is king of all English hearts even now, and the king will choose him to be his successor.

"It is a sore pity our king hath no son to succeed him," said Hilda.

"Nay, but our earl will make a better king than any son of Edward's," said Gurth warmly. "Surely thou hast not sold thy soul wholly to the Church," he added.

A faint smile broke over the invalid's face. "I have not sold myself to any, but I have given

SHIVER: *break in pieces*
TRAIN: *a moving line of people*

my heart to God and His Church," said the lady firmly.

Her brother started. "Hilda, thou hast done that, and broken thy promise!" he said.

"Nay, nay, my brother; I am here to welcome thee at all times, and it may be I shall never leave this house for the convent; but I could not but give my heart to God, and—"

"And become the slave of the Church!" interrupted Gurth fiercely.

"True, I must honour the Church and obey her laws; but I am no slave," said Hilda.

"Thou art, and 'tis slavery of the worst kind; for she imposeth her iron yoke upon all alike."

"It is but such a yoke and such a bondage as thou hast imposed upon Leofric," said Hilda.

"Nay, nay, Leofric is bound by no yoke; from the day I bought him the knave hath been free to leave me, if so he willed."

"Listen, now, and let me tell thee what the knave told me once, and thou shalt know then what the yoke is that binds me to God and the Church," said Hilda, drawing her brother nearer to her couch. "Gytha once feared that her brother had forsaken thee, and sought his freedom; and hearing that she had told me of these fears, he came to tell me how impossible it was for him ever to do this. 'My master bought me, redeemed me from the power of a cruel master, and told me I might serve him or leave him as I willed.

He wanted no slave-service from me, and would put no slave-badge upon me; but in that hour I felt he had taken my heart captive, and bound me to him with a bond stronger than links of iron.'"

Gurth smiled. "What hath that to do with thy selling thyself to the Church?" he said.

"Because the words of Leofric, and his love-service and heart-bondage to thee, doth show somewhat the way in which I am bound to serve God and obey His Church. Christ the Lord hath redeemed me from cruel slavery—the slavery of selfishness and sin. It was no small price He had to pay for my redemption, but His own blood, His own life. Gurth, think of it, my brother; nothing but the blood of Christ could redeem me —could wash away my sins. It was not a few crowns such as thou didst give for Leofric, but a life of privation and poverty, and a death of bitter agony and shame; and think you I could keep back my heart's love from such a Master? These are all the bonds He hath imposed, that I should love Him and pay Him such service as my poor heart can compass."

Her brother knew not what to say. In a less degree it was a similar feeling that bound him to the service of the great earl, and he would rather give up his life than forsake his master.

The wars, of which Hilda in her ignorance had spoken so lightly, soon called for the use of the

PRIVATION: *a lack of comforts and necessities*

weapons Gurth and Leofric had learned to handle; and they followed Harold to Wales in his war with the Welsh King Gryffyth, who aimed at nothing less than the throne of King Edward.

"And is Earl Harold afraid of losing his throne?" asked Gytha. "I heard my mistress talking to our lord her father yesterday, and it seems there is another who hath a right to the throne when our saint-king shall be taken to his rest."

"Saint-king!" repeated Leofric impatiently; "Edward is fit for a monk; he might have been a king if the Church had not spoilt him, as it spoils all men and women who learn to love its ways."

"Oh, Leofric, say not so!" answered Gytha quickly. "See what the love of God hath done for my mistress—see how much happier she is now! You would know the difference if you were one of her bower-maidens. And have we not worked for thee and thy master, and bought thee shirts of mail with the work of our fingers?"

"Yes, indeed, thou hast, little sister, and I meant not to speak ungratefully. It was not of thee I was thinking, but of this same saint-king, who wastes the treasures of England in buying Romish rags and bones wherewith to endow the churches, instead of repairing the ruined defenses of his kingdom."

"But—but he gives bountiful alms to the poor,

I have heard," said Gytha, seeking some excuse for
the king.

"Yes, yes; laying up treasure for himself in
heaven, he says, which is only another kind of
selfishness, I take it. Better do his duty as a
king, and set these same beggars to work on the
strong houses and timbered stockades that are
falling into ruins, and there would be fewer robbers infesting the woods. I tell thee, little sister,
Edward may be king in Westminster, but Earl
Harold rules England by right of doing his duty,
and loving England better than himself."

"But what is it men are talking of just now?
Edgar the Ætheling hath the right to the throne,
and if—"

But Leofric would not stay to listen to one
word against the great earl, but hurried on to
the great hall, where master and servants were
already assembling for the midday meal. Four
meals a day, and they neither light nor scanty,
and all served with plenty of wine or ale, were
what our Saxon forefathers looked upon as their
needful daily food; and they often ate to repletion, and drank until they fell under the tables,
helpless. To retire before this consummation had
been attained would have been looked upon as
cowardice, or, what was scarcely less disgraceful,
un-English. So Leofric soon forgot his sister's
words in the business of eating and drinking,
and would probably have sat some time longer

ÆTHELING: *an Anglo-Saxon prince or nobleman, especially
the heir to the throne*
REPLETION: *being abundantly or excessively filled*

than he did, but he saw his master rise from his seat, and motion to him as he left the hall, and Leofric instantly followed.

"Hast heard the news?" asked Gurth as soon as the two young men were outside.

"What news, my noble master?" asked Leofric.

"That Earl Harold will disappoint the secret but dearly-cherished hope of his thanes, and hath persuaded the king to acknowledge Edgar the Ætheling as his successor."

"Then that is what my sister heard the Lady Hilda talking of."

"Yes; my father hath been to reason with the earl against this, but Harold argues that it is for England's weal, if the lad shall be found a fit and proper boy. Leofric, this is the trick of the Church to be rid of a strong and able king, that it may rule or ruin England as it hath done of late. Nay, there is no questioning this, for Aldred, the Archbishop of York, doth openly speak of the Ætheling's right."

Leofric's love for the Church was no greater than his master's, and he was ready to look upon every evil as the fault of some of its ministers, or of those who professed to be guided by the dictates of religion. Even the great earl himself, almost faultless in the eyes of his followers, was blamed for his supposed leaning towards the Church; and now this news about the Ætheling

CONSUMMATION: *completing in every detail*
WEAL: *well-being, prosperity*

succeeding King Edward confirmed the suspicions of the earl's weakness in this direction.

"What saith the thane Godrith, thy father, to this choice of the Ætheling?" asked Leofric.

"He is ready to blame Earl Harold for placing himself under the teaching of the Church at all. Better have kept to the old gods, and trusted to our battle-axes, if need be. Another thing hath displeased my father, as it will do many others: our earl is not English in his manner of eating and drinking, and he hath even ventured to say we might copy those Norman thieves with advantage."

"Take pattern by the Normans! An Englishman learn of a Norman!" exclaimed Leofric indignantly.

"Well, it was fashionable to do this a few years ago," laughed Gurth. "We cut our beards and gowns after their pattern, but our appetite is another matter. Englishmen won't leave the table until they are well-filled, or let the wine-cup pass while they can hold it in their hands."

It was not often that Gurth found fault with the earl's doings or opinions, but upon this last matter he had once or twice fallen under the earl's displeasure for doing what was so common that men took it as a matter of course—rendering himself incapable of duty when that duty was imperative.

How often the great earl had been compelled

to speak seriously to others as well as Gurth—
how his campaign in Wales had been imperiled
again and again through this national vice, he
alone could tell; but he knew that it made him
distrust his most tried friends—not their faith, or
their courage, but their power to do their duty
when it was needed.

His sister, too, had ventured to speak to him
about this; and when he defended himself by
saying that it was common and English, she had
retorted that England had better become Norman, if that would check the further growth
of the vice.

So, altogether, Gurth had a good cause for
complaint against the Church now, he thought;
since it had turned his sister and his master
against him, and he was cross and moody, but
did not try to overcome his bad habits.

Every month things seemed to grow more un-
settled; and before the business of the succession
was completed, Earl Harold was sent for by his
brother Tostig to quell a rebellion in his earldom
of Northumbria. Their old family foes of Mercia
had taken up arms in favour of the rebels, so that
half England was ready to plunge into civil war,
and Harold called upon his thanes and lithsmen
to help him, in the name of the king and the law,
to put an end to this anarchy. But when the
messenger arrived to summon Gurth, he was
snoring and insensible, and half a dozen of his

LITHSMEN: *mercenary troops from the shipmen's guild*

friends lay with him outside the great hall, where the servants had dragged them when they cleared the tables away.

Leofric was not quite so bad as his master, and retained sense enough to comprehend the man's message; and knowing that Gurth would forgive anything rather than that he should not be made aware of what had happened, Leofric staggered to where a bucket of water stood not far off, and plunging his head in to sober himself, then carried it to where his master lay, and dashed it over him.

Gurth started up with an oath, scarce knowing where he was; but seeing Leofric with the bucket in his hand, and finding himself drenched with the water, he flew at him, snatched the bucket away, and dashed it at his head.

It was all done so quickly, that before either of his friends who had shared in the sousing could raise themselves, Leofric lay stretched upon the ground, bleeding from a deep wound in his forehead. The sight of the blood completely sobered Gurth, and he ran to help him up; but to his dismay Leofric showed no signs of life— neither spoke nor moved—and his white face looked ghastly against the fast-flowing blood as it fell in a pool beside him.

SOUSING: *drenching*

Chapter IX

Sickness

URTH had been on the field of battle, and had encountered death in its most ghastly forms, but his heart stood still with fright and horror as he leaned over Leofric.

"I must have been mad to do it," he gasped; and then he shouted for help, and one or two servants ran out to see what had happened. They looked horrified when they saw poor Leofric; but Gurth had no patience with their fright. "Lift him up, and carry him in, and one of you that is skillful in dressing wounds, bind up his head."

"Better send to the convent of St. Mary, and ask Father Alred to come. He is a skillful leech, as well as—"

"Do as I bid ye," thundered Gurth; "*I* will have no help from the Church, and no monk shall come here by my will."

"But, my master, he may die," one of the frightened maid-servants ventured to say.

"Let him die, then," said Gurth sullenly, and

trying to appear unmoved; for he was ashamed to let his father's house-carles see how deeply his heart was wrung by what had happened.

Leofric was carried to the little lean-to, where his master slept; and when his wound was dressed Gurth sat down beside the bed, and gave way to unavailing grief. He would not have it known for all that he possessed, but he actually burst into tears as he leaned over and gazed into Leofric's unconscious face.

Something in the unwonted sound seemed to rouse Leofric's dormant senses, and he said faintly, "Have they told thee the earl's message?"

"The earl's message?" repeated Gurth. "There, there, thou art dreaming, I can see, my poor fellow; try to go to sleep again, and we will talk of this by and by."

But instead of trying to go to sleep, Leofric struggled to raise himself on his elbow.

"My master, thou must go; every minute is precious. Oh, why could not some of the knaves have told thee why I threw the water over thee? they might have known."

"Oh, why didst thou play me that sorry joke? I had almost forgotten it again," said Gurth, glancing at his dripping garments.

"It would have been a sorrier joke to let thee sleep on, when Earl Harold hath summoned all his men to follow him to Northumbria," said Leofric, struggling against his weakness until he

UNWONTED: *rare or unusual*
DORMANT: *sleeping*

could convince his master that this was no idle
fancy of his brain.

Gurth was half-convinced now, and, starting
to his feet, began to unfasten his tunic at the
throat. "Earl Harold hath summoned us to go
with him to Northumbria," repeated Gurth; "was
that what the messenger said, Leofric?"

"Yes, yes, and time is precious," said Leofric
faintly.

Gurth threw off his dripping garments, and
went in search of his father, who had doubtless
received the messenger.

"Well, sluggard, I was preparing to go in thy
place," said the old thane, as his son entered the
great hall, where the servants had already begun
furbishing his arms to be in readiness.

"Thou hast news from Earl Harold," said
Gurth, with a glance at the gleaming armour.

"Yes, he hath summoned his lithsmen to follow
him to the field again."

"And Leofric cannot go with me," said Gurth
sadly.

"Is he dead?" asked Godrith, with assumed
carelessness; for he did not wish to add to his
son's grief if the slave had died.

"Nay, nay, I hope he will live to follow me to
other wars, though he cannot go now to Northumbria," said Gurth. "But why did the messenger delay his coming until the meal was over,
and our heads were full of strong ale? He might

surely have known that men were little fit to think of any business at this hour of the day," grumbled the young man, who felt vexed with himself, and therefore only too ready to throw the blame on someone else.

The old thane laughed at his son's vexation. "Nay, nay, blame not the messenger, but the ale, Gurth, for this mischance," he said. "Earl Harold will tell thee it is the wine and strong ale that causeth half the mischances too."

But Gurth was in no humour to be told of this just now, and so, after a few words with those who were to go with him, he hurried away to his sister's bower to bid her farewell and ask her to send Gytha to see that her brother was properly cared for by the house-carles.

"Why, what aileth Leofric?" asked Hilda, while Gytha turned pale with alarm.

Gurth turned away confused and half-ashamed. "I have struck him down and wounded him for playing me what I thought was a sorry joke," he said.

"Oh, Gurth, thou didst drown thy wit in the ale-horn again," said his sister, in a half-reproachful tone.

"And what if I did?" demanded Gurth angrily. "Am I not an Englishman? Wouldst thou have me a Norman shaveling?"

"O Gurth, thou knowest I love all things English; but if, as I have heard, these Normans are

---

SHAVELING: *used as an insult; refers to a monk or priest with a shaved area on the top of his head*

temperate in eating and drinking, ruling themselves wisely in this matter, it would be better
for thee and for all to follow their example."

"What! an Englishman learn of a Norman!
Fie on thee, Hilda. Hast thou so soon forgotten
thy Danish ancestors?"

"I cannot forget them when I see thee and the
best and bravest of our house-carles drinking till
ye have no more sense than swine."

So the brother and sister parted in anger—a
circumstance that Gurth soon forgot in the bustle
and excitement of the march northwards; but to
Hilda, in her quiet retirement, it was a source of
deep pain, and caused her many sleepless nights;
for what if Gurth never returned from this campaign?—and that her brave brother would rush
into the thick of the fight she knew quite well.

"If I had but spoken more gently he would
not have left me as he did," sighed Hilda again
and again. "If I could but remember Gytha's
message—Gytha's message," she repeated. "Nay,
nay, is it not my message too? Surely that was
what the old monk meant—that all who learned
this wondrous, blessed truth, that 'God is love,'
should tell it to another, that the news may
travel on and on, like the light of our beacon
fires that tells of danger at hand to the next, which
instantly springs into life and light, passing the news onward until all the country is
aroused. Yes, yes, Gytha's message shall be mine

TEMPERATE: *self-controlled*

too, and I will try to speak in love, and not in anger. Oh, if Gurth may but return from this campaign, I will give my life to sending this message abroad."

Gytha was almost as angry as her mistress when she went to see her brother and found him suffering from the dangerous wound on his head. As Gurth was out of the way, and could make no further objection to the learned monk being sent for, some of the servants had been to the convent of St. Mary and fetched this skilled leech to see Leofric, for his condition puzzled them, and the monk himself said he could scarcely understand the wound causing such a distemper of the whole body.

He bade Gytha watch her brother closely, and give him nothing but the cooling drink one of the sisters from the convent would bring.

"But he is always asking for ale; he bade one of the house-carles take me away from him, if I could not bring him a horn of strong ale," said Gytha tearfully.

"Ah, he had been drinking this same strong ale when his master struck him," said the monk quickly; and he knew at once what ailed his patient, and how small was his chance of recovery. But he would not tell Gytha this just now. Let the girl hope for the best as long as she could; but he said, as he left, "No more double ale, mind; but the decoction I will send,

DISTEMPER: *illness*

and a little water from the spring, and some barley bread, and a few grapes, if he is hungry."

Gytha stared, and thought her brother would be starved on such poor diet, but she promised to obey the monk's directions.

It was no easy task, however, to make Leofric obey her. The fever ran high, and he was very thirsty, but refused to touch the herb-tea sent by the sisters from the convent; but begged and prayed Gytha to fetch him a horn of ale, and threw himself into a violent passion when he found she would not go. Then he would try coaxing, pleading, and reproaches, telling her she could not love him as she once did, or she would not treat him so cruelly now he was ill and could not help himself. It was hard for Gytha to be told this, when she was doing all she could to relieve her willful brother; and she said to him rather tearfully, "Leofric, it is because I do love thee that I refuse to give thee this—because I know it will do thee harm."

Leofric flung himself over, displacing all the skins that Gytha had so neatly arranged on his bed. "Don't talk to me about love," he said, "when thou dost refuse to do as I wish."

"But, Leofric, thou art ill, and I want thee to get well again," said Gytha gently.

"Don't I want to get well? Dost think I want to die like a cow in my bed? I must journey to Northumbria, I tell thee, and take the blows that may be falling; an thou wilt give me a draught of good double ale I might begin my journey tomorrow," he added coaxingly.

But Gytha remained firm. "I can give thee something better than ale," she said; "something that will help thee to get over this distemper, so that thou mayst set out on thy journey without fear or danger to thy health."

"Naught will do this, I tell thee, but a bucket of our good English ale. I would that I could get forth to the kitchen; thou shouldst see then what I would do;" and Leofric fumed and tossed about, and was altogether as unmanageable a patient as any nurse was ever troubled with.

Some of the house-carles, when they heard Leofric calling for the ale, tried to persuade Gytha that it would be better to let him have it. "Thou wilt have no peace or rest thyself, if thou dost not give it to him."

"I care not for my own peace, but for my brother's life; and I believe what Father Alred hath told me—that he drinks too much ale, and it is this as much as his wound that hath caused this distemper."

"But he will wear thee out with these wild ravings. I should give it to him for the sake of peace," said the man.

Gytha smiled. "But he is not thy brother," she said; and when Leofric called for drink again, she ventured to take him the horn of herb-tea which she had at hand, and put that to his lips. But the moment he had tasted it he spat it out again, and pushed Gytha roughly aside.

"How canst thou give me such filthy stuff to drink?" he exclaimed; "it is bitter, and compounded of all evil things."

"Nay, nay, Leofric; it is a cooling drink prepared by the hands of the good sisters of St. Mary, and will cure thee of thy sickness and wound too."

"That—that cure me!" exclaimed Leofric; "why, 'tis enough to turn my blood to gall. Much thou knowest of what would cure mine ailments," he said contemptuously.

"Nay, nay, I said not that I did, Leofric; but good Father Alred is the most skillful leech between here and London, and he doth know for certain what will cure thy distemper."

"Then let Father Alred keep his cure, if he can give me no pleasanter drink than that;" and he made another wry face at the recollection of the disagreeable draught he had tasted.

When the doctor came the next day and found his patient no better, and the herb-tea almost untouched, he scolded Gytha for not giving it to her brother.

"Nay, nay, it is not her fault, holy father," said Leofric; "I would not take thy bitter draught."

"Then I can do nothing for thee, and thou

must die," said the monk, rising from the stool where he had seated himself at the bedside of his patient.

"Die—die like a cow in my bed and not on the battlefield, where every free-born Englishman would fain give up his life!" exclaimed Leofric.

"An thou art not brave enough to swallow a draught of herb-tea because it is bitter, thou dost deserve to die like a cow," said the monk coolly.

Leofric winced at these words. "No man ever questioned my valour before," he said. "Give me thy vile decoction, monk;" and the next minute he had swallowed the whole of it, unpleasant as it was.

"Drank like a hero," said the monk admiringly; "thou art worth making it even a little more bitter," he added.

"And wherefore should it be more bitter, holy father?" asked Leofric, somewhat appeased by the monk's last words.

"Well, my son, in this particular decoction the more bitter it is the more costly it is, and the better chance thou wilt have of being cured of thy distemper. If I cared not whether thou didst get well or die, I could make thee a drink pleasant as honey; but I have heard of thee and thy bold master Gurth Godrithson, and England may yet need every true man she can muster, and so I would fain save thee to strike a blow at England's foes if ever it should be needed."

"Well, thou dost speak fair, good father, but an I take thy vile bitterness, wilt thou not let me have some good ale? I have had not a drop since I have been here."

"And if thou didst never drink a horn of it again thou wouldst be the better man, I trow," said the monk boldly.

"An Englishman, and drink no ale!" exclaimed Leofric in astonishment.

"Well, I suppose it is asking too much; but I tell thee this is England's curse and England's danger—this want of moderation in eating and drinking."

"Surely thou art a Norman to speak thus of our good old English customs," exclaimed Leofric.

"They were Danish, I trow, before they were English," said the monk quietly.

"Ah, marry were they, and right proud should we be of them. Why, monk, thou shouldst see an Englishman and a Norman at meat together; the mean, pitiful, half-starved Norman!" added Leofric contemptuously.

"Ah, the Englishman would eat twice as much, and drink three times as much," said the monk.

"Three times! say five or six times, good father, and it were nearer the mark," answered Leofric triumphantly.

"Ah, I doubt it not," said the monk sadly.

MARRY: *an exclamation, used to express amused or surprised agreement*

"The Normans have learned to rule themselves—to eat not beyond what is reasonable, nor to drown their minds, which they are learning to use, in the wine-cup or ale-horn."

"The miserable, pitiful Normans! Prate not to an Englishman of them or their fashions, or aught that they do."

"Nay, but thou wilt find they are not to be despised, an it comes to another trial than that of appetites."

"Well, well, good father, I see thou art more than half a Norman, although thou dost look like a jolly good Englishman."

"It is because I am an Englishman, and would fain see England rise to be the great nation she might be, that I desire to see thee and all men using greater temperance in this matter of eating and drinking," said the monk seriously.

But Leofric only laughed. "Englishmen will learn nothing from any, except it be from their kinsmen the Danes. As for these Franks, and Normans, and men of Flanders—well, thou and thy fellow-monks may prate an ye will, but we will have nought to do with them," said Leofric contemptuously.

Of course he was only giving voice to the opinion of his master in speaking so disdainfully of foreigners, but the opinion or prejudice was not by any means confined to Gurth. The popular opinion upon this matter was very much the same;

PRATE: *babble or talk endlessly*

and left to themselves, the Englishmen, or Saxons, as they may at this period be called, would have kept England out of the reach of civilization, or at least she would have remained ages behind the neighbouring countries of Europe.

Chapter X

News From Oxford

EOFRIC was ill for several weeks, mainly owing to his restless impatience to get up, and rebellion against the doctor's orders, and during this time his sister nursed him with unwearied patience.

Leofric took this very much as a matter of course at first, but one day, when he had been more than usually trying—refusing to eat or drink anything that Gytha brought, and clamouring for double ale and a slice of boar's head, which had been specially forbidden by Father Alred—he suddenly turned to his sister and said, "Thou dost think I am little better than a boar myself; why dost thou not leave me and go to thy lady's bower?"

"Because thou dost need me here," said Gytha gently.

"But it cannot be pleasant for thee to stay here," said Leofric; "the Lady Hilda's bower is the best room in the house, and her maidens are always happy and merry now, they say."

"Yes, as thou sayest, there are no happier bower-maidens than the Lady Hilda's. God hath been very good to us, Leofric," Gytha ventured to say.

"Well, I know not what God hath had to do with the business, but 'tis certain thou hast a good mistress, and thou dost deserve it; and now thou hadst better go and enjoy thyself in her bower, and leave me."

But Gytha shook her head. "Thou wilt take no more of this good medicine an I leave thee," she said with a smile.

"And what if I did not? What could it matter to thee if I died now? The Lady Hilda would protect and befriend thee, and thou wouldst be far more comfortable in her bower than here listening to my grumblings."

"Nay, nay, Leofric, I could not be happy away from thee now. I do not mind the grumbling, except as it doth make thee worse to get into a passion."

The young man looked at his sister wonderingly. "It must be true, then, that thou dost love me, although thou dost seem unkind sometimes, Gytha."

"Unkind! Would it be kind to give thee what would harm thee, because thou dost clamour for it?" said Gytha. "Hast thou really doubted Gytha's love, my brother?" she asked tenderly.

"I—I do not doubt it now," he said evasively;

"I have been little better than a wild boar, and thou hast been very patient, Gytha, and hast never given me one angry word for all the ill names I have called thee. Yes, yes, I do believe thou lovest me now; but oh, if thou didst know how I have longed for a draught of our good ale, and how cruel it seemed to keep it from me, and —and thou didst sometimes laugh, and seem so cheerful, as though thou didst not care for me."

"But I did care a great deal," said Gytha, laughing again, in spite of herself. "Father Alred said thou wert doing well, and would do better if thou didst not fret and fume; and he bid me be cheerful to cheer thee."

Leofric could smile himself now at his mistake, but still his willfulness was not entirely conquered, and he often gave his sister a good deal of trouble, but he did not doubt her love, as he had done before.

His convalescence was the most wearisome time he had ever known. His wound was almost healed, but he was too weak to do more than crawl a few yards beyond the stockade and bask in the autumn sunshine. He was disappointed, too, that the campaign in Northumbria was over —or rather there had been no fighting at all; and Leofric wondered what the world was coming to, when men could miss such a fine opportunity for a battle, and choose to settle a dispute by appeal- ing to reason and justice, instead of the bow and battle-axe. That was what these degenerate Northumbrians had done—appealed to the known justice of their oppressor's brother and ally; and Earl Harold, although he had an army at his back, had listened to the rebels' complaint against his brother, saw that they had just cause for their murmurs, and settled the dispute without a blow being struck, although he gave mortal offense to his brother Tostig by so doing.

This was the news brought by the men of the earl's army who had returned home, many of them grumbling and dissatisfied because of their bootless errand.

But Leofric's young master had not yet come. He was staying with Earl Harold at Oxford, and it was uncertain when he would return, which was no pleasant news to Leofric, who was heartily tired of an idle life.

It seemed that affairs of great moment were to be transacted at Oxford, for the king and all the members of the Witan were journeying thither, as well as the bishops and abbots, and the principal men of Wessex. Leofric half-hoped that the old thane would have taken him with his retinue of house-carles; but Godrith never thought of bidding his son's slave journey to his master when he could have holiday at home, and so with ill-concealed vexation and disappointment Leofric saw the train depart.

Gurth was hardly less disappointed than Leofric

DEGENERATE: *low*
BOOTLESS: *useless, unprofitable*
MOMENT: *importance*

himself when his father reached Oxford without
his favourite henchman, and as soon as the principal business was settled he rode home with all
speed to tell the news.

Leofric was the first to meet and welcome his
master, and Gurth was so overjoyed to see him
that, jumping off his horse, he embraced him as
he would a brother, and then bade him follow him
to his sister's bower, where he was going to tell
the best news he ever had to relate.

All the household was astir with the tidings
that their young master had arrived, and as many
as dared pressed into the Lady Hilda's bower, for
that had grown to be the center of the household
—the meeting-place for telling news and discussing family questions.

The tidings of her brother's arrival had scarcely
reached Hilda when Gurth himself burst into the
room, his favourite hawk on his wrist, and two
or three dogs and half the household at his heels.

Such an invasion of her carefully rush-strewn
floor would have made Hilda peevish and irritable
at one time, but she had learned to consider
others now; and she rather liked to see the house-
carles come into her room to hear the family
news.

So she greeted the whole turbulent party with
a smile when they rushed into the room after
Gurth, only bidding Leofric take care that his
master's dogs did not fly at her maidens, and

bidding the girls stop their spinning for awhile now that her brother had come.

"Why, Gurth, thou art as much a boy as ever," she said, as her brother leaned over her couch, and kissed her again and again. She smoothed back the long golden hair that lay in clustering curls upon his shoulders, and looked into his merry blue eyes with a world of content in her gaze, for she could see that her brother had thought no more of the anger in which they had parted, and she would not disturb him by referring to it just now.

"So, lady sister mine, thou dost think I am a boy again," said Gurth gaily, as he gazed at the heavy gold bracelets on his wrists, and the gown which was his usual holiday attire, but which he had been too impatient to change for a plainer dress when he left Oxford. "Now what wilt thou give me for my news, lady sister?—the best news England could hear, it is mine to tell."

"Is it of Earl Harold?" asked Hilda, who shared in her brother's admiration of the great earl.

"Yes, yes; he is to be crowned King of England!" exclaimed Gurth; and turning to the house-carles, he said, "Now shout for King Harold, true Englishman and noble knight!"

They needed no second bidding to do this, and none shouted longer or louder than Leofric; but before it was over Hilda raised her face to her brother again.

"Gurth, Gurth, what of King Edward?" she said.

"Oh, he is well," said Gurth lightly; "that is, he is dying slowly, and will leave the throne for his noble successor in a few months."

Hilda looked pained at this. "I cannot bear to hear thee talk of our saint-king in this heedless fashion, and to set the witless knaves shouting for Earl Harold, as though he were already king, was no good thing to do," she said.

"Nay, nay, be not angered, Hilda; but if thou knewest all—how Earl Harold doth work for the good of England—thou wouldst not grudge him being king in name, as he hath long been in the hearts of all true Englishmen."

"Nay, nay, I grudge him not the honour of kingship, Gurth, but I would have thee more cautious how thou dost set about proclaiming the earl as king; for it will mightily displease King Edward an it cometh to his ears. But this choice of Harold is somewhat sudden, I trow. It was but a few weeks since thou didst tell us that the great earl and Bishop Aldred were for securing the right of Edgar the Ætheling."

"Yes, yes; and had he proved a proper little knave, and likely to make a king worthy the name, he would have been proclaimed by the Witan; but Duke William the Norman doth claim our English crown, and 'twere useless to set up a puppet like the Ætheling against him.

But who could find a better, truer, nobler man than Harold? Even his foes say this; and not a churchman could say he ever burned a convent, or took a hide of abbey land. Nay, nay, the only quarrel our great earl hath with the Church is, that too much money is spent in relics and such like rubbish, that might and ought to be expended in the defenses of our coasts."

"But, Gurth, Edward is a good king," said Hilda.

"He hath done little harm, I grant thee; but, Hilda, that is not enough in these days," said Gurth.

"Not enough! To be good, not enough!" said Hilda.

"Well, well, I forgot I was talking to one who believes with the Church that her own soul is of such countless price that all others may be sacrificed for it;" and with this half-sneering remark Gurth was about to turn away, but his sister caught hold of his gown and detained him.

"Gurth, thou art making a great mistake," she said earnestly. "The Church doth not teach us to be selfish, but to be tender and mindful of the good of others."

"How canst thou say that, when she is always teaching, that if men and women want to save their souls, they must leave the world, and all their friends who do the work of the world, and retire to a convent? Thou, too, art like the rest;

thou dost pine for the convent," said Gurth fiercely.

"But—but it was not because I desired to leave thee, but because the convent seemed the only place for a poor helpless woman like me."

This reference to her condition quite subdued her brother's anger, and he said in a gentler tone, "Thou art not helpless, Hilda; for if thou canst do little for thyself, thou doest much for others. Why, thou art the heart and soul of the household, and how could we spare thee to go to the convent? It rouses my anger whenever I think of it."

"Then do not think of it," said his sister with a smile; "for I have promised to stay here as long as thou shalt need me."

"To escape the first time thou hast a decent excuse for doing so," said Gurth laughing.

"Nay, then, I promise this, to stay until thou dost bid me go to the convent," said Hilda solemnly.

"Now thou art my own sister, and ever wilt be," said Gurth, kissing her fondly. "I know I shall never bid thee go to the convent; but, Hilda, thou shalt learn some of the wisdom they teach there. I will get thee one of King Alfred's Books—the Saxon Scriptures, that thou mayst read to thy bower-maidens sometimes."

"Oh, Gurth!" was all the lady could utter for some time, for it seemed that, if she could only possess such a costly treasure as this, the world could have nothing else to offer.

"There, we will say no more about quarreling," interrupted Gurth; "thou shalt have the Book, and enjoy thy opinion about King Edward; only thou must give me the same liberty of belief: and I believe that a man who works when he can, and prays when he can't, is better than a man who is always praying, but never lifts his finger to help with the work. The last is King Edward—thy saint-king. Well, he may be a saint, but he is not a man; and God hath made the world for men, I trow, and they must work an they would live."

Hilda looked troubled, and somewhat puzzled how to answer her brother. King Edward was perfect, or nearer to perfection than any man on earth, and yet she heard every hour that it was the more practical and commonplace earl that England needed; and how could she make her brother believe that the precious relics upon which the king lavished so much of the national wealth were a greater safeguard than stockades, and wooden forts, and ships to protect their island-home?

There was, however, one work of King Edward's in which his subjects took a warm interest, and that was the building of the Westminster in the isle of Thorney, just beyond the village of Charing. This building, which had occupied years, and for which many foreign workmen belonging to the order of Masons had been brought over to direct the more ignorant native workmen, was fast approaching completion, and it was to be consecrated at Yuletide in midwinter; and Godrith, to please Earl Harold, resolved to take his family to Charing beforehand, that they might be present at the festival, which occupied so much of the king's thought and attention.

Earl Harold was about to be married to the daughter of his family foe, Leofric of Mercia, that the old feud might be healed, and England ruled as one nation. This had been settled at Oxford; but the news did not please Gurth, and so it was not until the old thane returned that Hilda heard this interesting item of intelligence.

"Why didst thou not tell me of Earl Harold and the Lady Aldytha?" she said to her brother, when he came into her bower one morning.

Gurth shrugged his shoulders with something like vexation. "Earl Harold hath no right to do this thing," he said; "he could give his time and labour for our merrie England, but he hath no right to give himself, as he hath done, in taking Aldytha to be the Lady of England instead of the Lady Edith, to whom he hath long been betrothed."

"But—but it may be—"

"Nay, Hilda, we will not talk of this. I am

MINSTER: *a large or important church*

vexed. I hold that the earl is wrong; but I would not hear another say this. Now tell me, art thou pleased that my father will carry us all to this Thorney minster at Yuletide?"

"Pleased!" exclaimed Hilda; "how canst thou ask me, when I have so often longed to go to church that I have often shed tears when I heard the bells ringing? And now, to think I am to see the great minster, the glory of England, for my father saith my litter shall be carried in, and set down in some quiet corner, where I may see the king and the bishops and the great altar. Oh, Gurth, it will be almost like heaven!" said Hilda, in an excited whisper.

Gurth nodded; but, truth to tell, he was looking forward to the feasting and carousing rather than the religious part of the ceremony; and speaking of this to Leofric afterwards, they agreed that women were religious dreamers, quite unfit for the everyday work of the world.

Chapter XI

At Charing

ERY bare and cheerless, according to our modern notions of comfort, was the mansion taken by Godrith, the Wessex thane, in the little village of Charing. An odd collection of substantially-built farmhouses formed the whole village, and one of the largest and best of these had been purchased by Godrith; for if Harold was to be king he would often have to be at court, and this village, situated between London and the little isle of Thorney, where the palace stood, was convenient for many reasons.

It was quite an event in the life of Hilda—this removal to Charing, for no one had thought of taking her beyond her own bower, since she had been brought there a little fretful girl of twelve, who cried and complained of the fatigue and pain she endured in being brought from her former home—an isolated farmhouse belonging to her father in a distant part of Wessex. The recollection of this journey was still fresh in her memory, and made her dread the removal to Charing more than she cared to own to anyone but her favourite bower-maiden Gytha. The story that her mistress related of that former journey, when she was laid in a wagon and drawn by oxen over the rough and ill-made roads, made Gytha almost shudder, and she resolved to see her brother and ask him if he could not devise a plan for carrying her beloved mistress in a less clumsy vehicle than a wagon.

Leofric was not devoid of inventive power when he had any motive for its exercise, but no one in those days thought of making life more pleasant or multiplying its domestic comforts. To eat and drink and sleep, fight and wrestle, was the aim and end of life, and those who thought it could be more than this were considered dreamers.

But now that Gytha had propounded the difficulty of removing her mistress—for of course she would not ride on horseback, as ladies usually did—Leofric set himself steadily to think out a plan by which it might be effected without causing the lady so much fatigue and suffering.

He broached the subject to his master; but Gurth had too many other things in his mind to give very much attention to this, so he bade Leofric set his wits to work and do anything he liked to give pleasure to his sister.

OWN: *admit*
PROPOUNDED: *presented for discussion or consideration*

The plan when thought of was simple enough, so simple that Leofric thought that they must all have been asleep for years not to have taken the lady out for many a pleasant summer ramble; for what would be easier than for the house-carles to carry her couch, while with a little contrivance, curtains might be stretched across from upright poles, to shelter her from the rain or sun, and screen her from the gaze of passengers on the road?

Hilda was delighted with the idea, and Gytha, of course, thought her brother wonderfully clever. The lady herself seemed to think him quite a genius, and readily promised to let him have the linen necessary for the curtains of her litter, and entered quite warmly into the discussion for affixing the upright posts to her little couch. The house-carles would carry it with the usual supports, and before the day of removal came Hilda went out for a trial trip.

It seemed to give her new life to be out in the open air, and though the trees were almost bare, for it was far on in the autumn now, she enjoyed the bright gleams of sunshine, and her mother seemed to enter into her daughter's pleasure, and declared she looked brighter and happier than she had been since she was a little girl.

The house-carles, shy and awkward at first, seemed to think they had a share in giving the lady this unwonted pleasure, and carried her as gently as possible, so that, when Hilda reached her bower again, instead of being fatigued and full of pains, she declared it was the happiest hour of her life, and she thanked the house-carles with tears in her eyes for the pleasure they had given her.

"Gytha, it was like what I should fancy being in a church must be," she said, when she and Gytha were left alone afterwards. "I could look right up into the blue sky, and see the white clouds sailing about the throne of God."

"Yes, heaven is God's throne, I suppose," said Gytha; "but I remember good Father Dunstan telling us once, that we should remember when we thought of the throne, that we were on the footstool,—not far from the throne."

"Nay, but what could he mean by that, my Gytha?" said the lady; "heaven is very far off."

"Not so far but this world is the footstool, the good father said, and he was a wise and learned monk—the wisest man in Bricstowe," added Gytha.

The lady looked puzzled for a few minutes, but at last she said, "If it be as thou sayest, and God is so near, verily I marvel that this world is so ill-managed, for not a day passes but we hear of some evil deeds. Gurth, my brother, told me but yesterday that a band of robbers had been seen here in our own pleasant greenwood, and but for our going to Charing so soon, he and the house-carles and ban-dogs would have hunted them further afield. It is not well that no honest man can pass near our dwelling without being robbed and beaten."

"But,—but there always have been robbers," said Gytha.

"But why should there be? If God can do all things, and this world is His footstool, surely things should not be as they are. Gytha, Gytha, I do not like to think of this world as God's footstool," added the lady sorrowfully.

"And wherefore not, dear lady? It is a sweet thought to me that we are about the feet of God now, though the saints and angels only see His face, except it be men like our King Edward, who is now dwelling more in heaven than on earth."

"Which accounts, perhaps, for the little heed he taketh of this poor kingdom of England, except to enrich it with the relics of saints, leaving its needful defenses to men like Earl Harold, who hath spent half the revenue of his earldom in doing what the king should have done."

"If it were not that our king is a saint, I should think it were better not to forget that we are on God's footstool in our eagerness to see His face, but to abide in patience here, doing what we can in our poor way to make the place of God's feet somewhat more like the heavens where His face shineth."

"Why, Gytha, that is only another way of saying what my brother spoke of only yesterday morn concerning the convents. He holdeth that it is selfish of good men and women to shut themselves out of the world."

"But the world liveth in wickedness," said Gytha.

"But thou sayest it is the footstool of God, and my brother saith if all the good monks and nuns would do their part to better it, as earnestly and truly as doth Earl Harold, the good and evil would be more fairly matched, and it might be that the good would conquer the evil at last."

But Gytha shook her head. "Thou dost not know the violence and cruelty of wicked men in the world," she said.

"But thou hast told me of it, Gytha—of the hard, cruel man who took thee as slave to Bricstowe market, and how the good old monk rescued thee, and overcame the man's evil nature by good. I have often thought of it—thought that Gurth might be partly right after all, in saying that the convents robbed the world; and now if, as thou sayest, it is God's footstool, and He hath given to each one who hath listened to His voice a message to his fellows, telling them He loves them, and would have them love Him —why, Gytha, half the messengers have hidden themselves, and buried the message instead of delivering it."

"But the people will not have it; they are all cruel and wicked," said the girl.

"Nay, nay, many of them have had small chance of hearing it," said the lady.

"But they can an they will—they can go to church. Listen now to the vesper-bells that are ringing; is not that God's call to the people to go and learn of His ways?" said Gytha earnestly.

"And dost thou not think I have often heard the vesper-bell without ever thinking of what it meant, or caring that I could not go to church? I doubt whether it can be the voice of God—it is only a church-bell to any soul until a living voice hath spoken to it, another soul taught it, that 'God is love.' Thou sayest the people hear the message, but in that thou doest them wrong, I ween. I was hard, and cold, and often cruel to my bower-maidens, but I was glad to hear thy message—God's message sent by thee. I could believe it, too, because thou didst show me something of the love in thy care and thoughtfulness for me, that didst not make me scornful of thy pity, as I was of all other."

A radiant smile beamed in Gytha's face as she leaned over her mistress' couch and whispered, "I could not help loving and pitying thee."

"Many pitied me before thou camest, Gytha, but few loved me, and it was thy tender love and compassion that made it possible for me to believe in the love of God. But the others are coming back now, and thou mayst go to thy supper;" and the next minute Gytha's companions entered the room, and she went to eat what they had chosen to leave for her at the supper-table.

Her position as the favourite bower-maiden of the Lady Hilda was rather an anomalous one, for she was a slave among these free-born Saxon maidens, each of whom took it as a personal insult that she should be treated by their mistress on an equality with them. She ought to be their slave, to do their bidding, and they thought themselves wronged every time she took up her distaff, or embroidery-needle, and seated herself among them. She had hoped that this feeling would change as time went on, but all her advances towards kindness and a more friendly state of feeling had been proudly repulsed.

Hilda knew something of this, and had spoken to the girls about it more than once, but she found they were not so much to be blamed as their friends. Whenever they went home this grievance of having a slave in the bower upon an equality with themselves was descanted upon, so that it was always rankling in their minds. They could not help liking Gytha; they owned to themselves she was kind and forbearing—good enough to be a nun; if she would only go to a convent, and free their lady's bower from her presence, they could almost love her. How much Gytha herself desired to enter a convent, and how disappointed she felt

ANOMALOUS: *abnormal, not what would be expected*
DISTAFF: *a staff used in spinning wool or flax*
RANKLING: *irritating*

every time her mistress spoke a disparaging word of those places, they did not know. It had been her hope for years now, that her mistress, having learned to love God, would quit her godless family, and in the stillness and quietness of the convent learn more of His love, and at length become a saint of renowned sanctity. Of course she would accompany her mistress when she went, but the chance of their going at all seemed to grow less as the time went on; and Gytha was both surprised and grieved that her mistress could be content to abide at home merely because her friends did not wish her to go.

There was no room here, Gytha thought, for the cultivation of those Christian graces that were needful before they could hope to be saints. Her mistress could never go to church, and she herself did not go so frequently as she could wish —never to more than one service during the day; whereas if they were nuns there would be five services in the church every day, to say nothing of other devotional exercises. Of course Hilda knew nothing of all these privileges, and she listened to, and more than half-believed, the stories Gurth told her of worldly bishops, who owned and traded in slaves; of rapacious priests, who cared nothing for their flocks but for the wool they could shear from them. True, she believed all Gytha told her of the teaching of Father Dunstan, and reverenced the old monk of Bric-

SANCTITY: *holiness*
RAPACIOUS: *extremely greedy*

stowe as much as she did Earl Harold; but the reverence in the two cases was too nearly allied to quite satisfy Gytha, for it was not the monk's fame for sanctity, but his kindness and active goodness, as well as the wise words that she had often repeated to her mistress, that drew forth the lady's reverence for the monk.

But now that Hilda could go out in her litter, Gytha hoped that she would often go to church, and, listening to the sweet voices of the nuns singing, surely she could not but wish to join the sisterhood. Hilda was quite as anxious as her bower-maiden to join in the public worship of God, and learn something more of His love; and she resolved to do so when they were once settled at Charing, although it would doubtless cause some surprise, and perhaps displeasure, that she should thus openly profess her attachment to God. Her family and friends prided themselves on their faithfulness to the old Norse deities, and still invoked Odin and Baldur; but in truth no religious belief of any kind troubled their minds beyond the superstitious fears and terrors that were common to all men, and which not even the Christian faith had been able to eradicate.

Of course the old heathen worship had long since passed away, but Hilda's friends chose to declare they were Odin's men still, and prided themselves in never entering a church, or obeying the word of either monk or bishop, so that it re-

ERADICATE: *root out*

quired no small courage for Hilda to declare herself a Christian. She had done this quietly and
unostentatiously for some time, and her mother
and father could not but own that there was a
wonderful change in their daughter, but they
scouted the idea that her Christian faith had
anything to do with this.

Godrith was going in the train of Earl Harold
to the consecration of the new minster, as he
would go to any other court festival;—it was
that to him and nothing more, and he had made
an effort to secure a sheltered nook in the sacred
edifice that his daughter might witness the great
show—the splendid dresses of the court and
bishops—for no other reason. That Hilda would
care nothing for all this finery—nay, that she
would rather have dispensed with it all as dis-
tracting her attention from the sublime thought
that this was God's house, the shrine which the
saint-king had been years in building, and would
now humbly pray the great God of heaven to
consecrate by His presence;—That King Edward
himself should feel something of this would be
quite intelligible to Godrith, for even he was not
without a share of the superstitious reverence in
which this last king of the royal line of Cerdic
was held by his subjects; but that his daughter
or any common mortal could know anything of
such an exalted feeling, he did not believe. It
was well that the world was different from their

UNOSTENTATIOUSLY: *not in a showy way*
SCOUTED: *rejected scornfully as absurd*
EDIFICE: *a large or massive building*

saint-king, or things would be worse than they were, he argued. One saint in the land was quite enough. The king was a living proof that when men became religious they were only fit to be shut up in a convent, for they were quite unfit to fulfill the everyday duties of life; and this Wessex thane was not alone in his opinion.

Chapter XII

The New Minster

ILDA had never seen London until she was carried through it in her litter that bright autumn day; her mother and father riding just before her, and her brother and Leofric in charge of the house-carles, who bore her light weight just behind. What a wonderful day that was to Hilda, for all that she had ever heard of London had little prepared her for the reality of the busy scene upon which they entered before they came to the great bridge lined with booths, and yet broad enough to allow two vehicles to pass. Here at Southwark she saw the two rings set apart for bear-baiting and bull-baiting, of which she had heard so much from Gurth. Once in the city, too, what strange sights and strange-looking people met her at every turn. Merchants from Germany, and dark-hued strangers from Africa, and Saracens of whom she had heard such strange tales from Gurth, for her brother had prepared her for some of these sights. Then, as they wound their way along the narrow crooked streets, darkened by the high timber-built houses, what wonders in the way of merchandise met her gaze in the little booths and stalls ranged outside the houses, and near which stood the cheap-men and merchants calling upon passengers to come and buy. Wherever one street crossed another there stood a holy rood or figure of some saint, and every few turns gave them a glimpse of some convent garden, so that these busy Londoners, she thought, could never plead as an excuse for not loving God that there was nothing to remind them of Him.

After passing out of Leodgate—the people-gate —and crossing the little bridge over the Fleet, they passed along the Strand, smooth sands stretching down to the river on the left, and green fields, with here and there a house just visible in the distance, and vineyards and gardens clustering round them.

By the time they reached Charing, which was within view of the lovely little isle of Thorney, which the saint-king had chosen for his new palace and minster, Hilda was quite wearied with the strange sights and sounds that had met her all along the route, and she felt no inclination to look for the new minster, which could be seen from the window of her bower. She possessed the unwonted luxury of a glazed window, the only one in the homestead in Kent, and the sash

CHEAP-MEN: *tradesmen*
ROOD: *a large crucifix or cross*

had been taken out and brought with them, or rather sent on before, by a skilled workman, to put in the aperture in her bower in place of the linen blind with which most of the houses were furnished.

But a busier and more exciting scene awaited Hilda in the consecration of the new abbey. From early morning the river was crowded with boats, while crowds of citizens came along the Strand, and all who could crossed to the little island where King Edward lived. There was no bridge here, and it was with difficulty that Hilda was ferried across; but at last she reached the shelter of the abbey, where she would rest and wait some hours before the ceremony began.

It was the first time Hilda had ever been in a church, and as her litter was set down in the dim far-off corner, which was the only space that could be spared for her, and she gazed along the row of Saxon arches and massive pillars, a feeling of awe crept over her, and she covered her face with her hands, murmuring, "At last, at last I am in the house of God;" and her heart was lifted in silent thanksgiving, and she too prayed as earnestly as King Edward that this house which he had build might stand forever as a glorious temple, where men and women might listen to the message He had sent, and which had brought such blessing to her life—that 'God is love.'

At last came the grand procession of bishops,

APERTURE: *an opening or hole*

priests, and monks, chanting sweet hymns as they walked along the aisles, and then the king himself, white-haired and looking prematurely old and worn, but with something of an exalted rapture in his face, and walking firmly forward, but as seeing nothing of all the outward pomp by which he was surrounded. Then Hilda caught a glimpse of the sweet patient face of the Lady of England herself, as the king's wife was then styled, and all that she had ever heard of her kindness and active goodness Hilda could well believe now, and how the king, saint as he was, could treat her with the coldness and neglect he did was a puzzle to her, as it had been to many others.

She saw, too, Earl Harold and his beautiful but haughty-looking countess, soon in her turn to be the Lady of England, the gossips said—although, looking at King Edward today there seemed little likelihood that his own prediction concerning his speedy death would be fulfilled, since he looked better than he had done for many months.

Of course a great banquet followed the ceremony of consecration, but Hilda saw nothing of this, for, as soon as the church was clear and their boat could be brought to the landing-place, she went home, glad to escape from the din and turmoil outside the church, and eager to tell Gytha something of the grand scenes she had witnessed.

The feasting and dissipation following on the consecration of the new abbey were scarcely over

DISSIPATION: *indulgence*

before the news was bruited abroad that the king was dying. He had ceased to take any notice of what was passing around him from the time he left the abbey church. With that consecration service his life in this world seemed to end, and men began to grow anxious once more about his successor. True, Harold had been chosen by the Witan at Oxford, but the crown had been claimed by Duke William of Normandy, who said it had been promised to him by King Edward, and traveling-merchants brought the news that Duke William was making preparations to enforce his claim. The question was resolving itself into this—Was England to be ruled by a foreigner, or by the man who had shown himself wise in counsel and brave in war, who loved his country better than himself? Gurth and Leofric would walk to London and mingle with the crowd of cheap-men and 'prentice lads, and propound this question to them in varied forms, but always receiving the same answer. Earl Harold should be their king if they could choose, and for once the popular voice carried some weight in the matter.

But to the relief of all save the Norman prelates, who were working in the interest of William, King Edward just before his death named Harold as his successor, and this was speedily confirmed by the Witan. What a fever and ferment pervaded everything from the time the

BRUITED: *reported*
PRELATES: *high church officials*

abbey was consecrated until Harold was crowned king! And then what shouting and joy followed!

Harold, the last of the Saxon kings, was crowned in the new abbey, and as soon as the crown was placed upon his brow the officiating bishop said, "We choose thee, O Harold, for lord and for king!" and then the thanes drew round, and, placing their hands upon the king's knee, shouted, "We choose thee, O Harold, for lord and for king!" and this taken up by the multitude inside the church, and re-echoed by the thousands outside, was borne across the little river, where crowds of others, gathered in the village, took up the glad triumphant strain, "We choose thee, O Harold, for lord and for king!"

The shouts reached Hilda's bower, and she, in a merry voice and no less gladsome heart, said to her maidens, "Come, lay aside the distaff for to-day, and let us shout for the king as well as the lusty knaves outside."

Of course there was feasting and revelry everywhere, and if Duke William had made a descent upon London that night he would have been master of the city before morning, for scarcely a man was sober enough to know what he was about, except a few attendants of those who had been to the royal banquet. In the cold gray dawn of that wintry morning a row of Saxon and Danish nobles sat propped against the palace wall, sleeping off the effects of their deep potations

LUSTY: *full of life, joyous*
POTATIONS: *alcoholic drinks or brews*

of the night before, and watched over by their surly sleepy attendants.

The festivities were not over the second day, or the third, but gradually the city and the court subsided to something like its normal condition, and King Harold set himself to examine the state of his finances with a view to strengthening his forts and defenses, for news had come that his brother Tostig was seeking help from their old foes the Danes, to regain his earldom of Nor-thumbria. That William, Duke of the Normans, would also make an attempt to invade the land was only too probable, and the two attacks might be made at the same time.

In the great hall of Godrith the work of fur-bishing arms went on all day long, while in the bower of Hilda the maidens spun and embroidered with quick and dexterous fingers, that the mer-chants of London might exchange the work of their needles and distaffs for bows and battle-axes, steel corslets and shields.

But, in spite of the busy industry and the chill creeping fear that would make itself felt some-times, this was a very happy spring to Hilda. She could go to the church of the neighbouring convent whenever it was fine—her family had made less opposition to this than she had ex-pected,—and then she often spent several hours of the day in the pleasant garden that sloped down to the edge of the river, where she could watch the boats of the citizens and courtiers passing up and down the stream.

Gurth had brought her the promised treasure, a copy of the Saxon Scriptures, in which she could read for herself the record of God's love, and now, reclining on her couch in the midst of her busy bower-maidens, she often read to them a portion of God's Word, bidding them treasure it in their hearts, and tell to others the message His Son had come to make known to men, that 'God is love.' To Gytha it was almost like being a nun this happy, busy springtime. The religion of that age forbade her thinking that any life, however useful, could be quite so good as the poorest one spent within the shadow of the convent. That her mistress did not share this belief to the full extent Gytha wished, was mainly owing to the fact that she knew so little about the outward forms of religion, and had thus escaped many of the mistakes made by some of the best and holiest people. God loved her—had loved her in spite of affliction that made her almost despicable in the eyes of the strong and robust, thought Hilda—loved her in spite of her fretful unhappy temper—nay, had loved her out of it, for the thought of this love had conquered the fretful unhappiness; and now, in the gladness of her heart, she was anxious that all should know and receive this love; and that Gytha's message should be passed on to others who had not heard it. But how could this be done in the convent, shut out from the world and those who needed to learn this message? This was the question Hilda had been asking herself lately—especially since her talk with Gytha about this world being God's footstool.

She had talked to Gurth about this, and had once or twice induced him to stay and listen to her reading something from the Book he had brought her, but it was not often she could get him to stay long enough for this. It was no time for dalliance in ladies' bowers, he said, when England was threatened with two invasions, and such scant tidings could be gleaned of the movements or preparations of the foe.

So when not engaged in looking after the making and furbishing of arms, Gurth, with his faithful attendant Leofric, went to the mart to see if any merchants had newly arrived from Flanders or Normandy, and could tell him anything of what was going on there; or else he would go to the butts near Newington, with a party of his father's house-carles, to practice archery. These duties and pastimes, with the necessary attendance at court, filled Gurth's time now, and Hilda was pleased to know that there were fewer scenes of drunkenness in the great hall, and her brother rarely drank so much but that he could walk from the table instead of rolling underneath it.

DALLIANCE: *wasting time*
MART: *fair or market*
BUTTS: *mounds or banks used for target practice*

Pity that it was not always so—that men could not at all times find occupation for mind and hand. But it could not be, she thought with a sigh. This season of feverish industry and excitement would pass. The Count of the Normans, and the Danes under Tostig, would be driven back, and the conquering army would come home and sink back into its former habits of gluttony and intemperance.

It was not greatly to be wondered at either if they should, thought Hilda, for the great hall where master and servants, dogs and hawks, lived and ate and slept, with rushes on the floor that were not changed more than twice a year, except to have another layer sprinkled over them, was to her a very unsavoury place.

Her mother laughed when Hilda had once ventured to say as much, and suggested that the rushes should be changed more frequently.

"Thou art over-fastidious, Hilda," she said. "Thou hast lived here in thy bower with thy maidens in the midst of such luxury that thou wouldst fain persuade us it is needful. Nay, nay, child, 'twere a waste of good rushes, and the dogs rake up many an old bone that would have been lost an I followed thy plan of having all new rushes laid once a month."

"I know thou dost think me wasteful in the matter of rushes," said Hilda.

"Nay, nay, I said not a word about it now;

OVER-FASTIDIOUS: *having excessively delicate standards*

the knaves have orders always to keep a good store of rushes for thy bower, for thou hast little enough to make life pleasant to thee;" and the lady sighed.

Hilda did not notice the sigh. "But—but I have been thinking of late, my mother, that if life could be made pleasant for all it might be better—if the great hall could be made pleasant as my bower now," said Hilda, looking round at the tapestry on the walls, and the glass window that afforded a pleasant outlook upon the garden and river beyond.

Her mother looked at the window too, and then at Hilda in unfeigned astonishment.

"Thou wouldst have every house-carle live like a king, Hilda—fresh rushes, windows, and wall-riff—what next?" asked the elder lady.

"It would cost less than the eating and drinking to excess," said Hilda, "and might help them to overcome it in time."

The lady shook her head. The notion was too wild even to be seriously talked about; but it was laughed over among the house-carles afterwards as a good joke, for they had overheard their mistress telling her husband and son of Hilda's plan for curing the men of drunkenness.

UNFEIGNED: *genuine*
WALL-RIFF: *literally "wall-rubbish," refers to decorations on the walls*

Chapter XIII

The Battle of Hastings

HE king's unnatural brother soon made good his threat of revenge by ravaging the south coast of England. But being beaten back by the forces of the king he betook himself to the eastern shore and mouth of the Humber.

The summer passed in the midst of stormy disquiet, but nothing more was heard of Duke William since the sending an ambassador to claim the crown, which had been refused, and when autumn came round again people had begun to grumble at the needless trouble and expense they had incurred in preparing for an enemy who was never likely to come.

Godrith had taken his family back to their home in Wessex, for the harvest claimed his attention, and he, like the rest, began to smile at the idea of an invasion by the Normans. "They had driven off Earl Tostig, and that had frightened the shaveling Normans from making attempt to invade the land," he said confidently.

But before the harvest was well-gathered this dream was rudely broken. Not from the south, but from the north came the herald of war. Their old and dreaded foes, the Danes, had landed once more, and ravaged all the land to York. Hastily every man armed; Gurth and Leofric, as well as the old thane, joined the king's army, and his wife at once declared her intention of following her lord to the battlefield. Hundreds of Saxon matrons would go too, following in the wake of the army, to be at hand should such succour as they could render be needful, or to have the last comfort of rescuing their dead from the heaps of slain.

When Hilda heard of her mother's intention she burst into tears. "Oh that I might go with thee, my mother!" she exclaimed.

"Nay, nay, Hilda, thou must stay with thy maidens, and see that the few house-carles we can leave take good care of the house, and gather in what remains of the harvest," said Lady Elfrida.

"But—but if I were only strong as other maidens I could go with thee, for who will comfort thee if—"

"Nay, nay, I shall need no comfort: I am but going to see the victory. Thou dost forget that the king goes with his army, and whenever did Harold, the earl, lose a battle? and shall Harold, the king, do less valiantly? I tell thee, Hilda, he is a host in himself."

"Yes, yes, I have heard my father say he is king, and state, and heart of England: then should he go with the army to expose a life so precious?"

"Nay, nay, Hilda, these are weak womanly fears, unworthy the daughter of thy father. The king will ensure a victory by his presence. Now, look well to the maidens while I am gone, and before thou dost expect us we shall be back;" and, saying this, Lady Elfrida left the room.

"Oh, Gytha, if we were not helpless maiden folk, we too, could go to the battle," said Hilda, trying to comfort her bower-maiden and herself too, for Gytha was as much troubled by the separation from Leofric as her mistress was at parting with her mother, father, and brother.

"I have been thinking the same thing," sobbed Gytha. "If I could but go to the battle—" but at this moment she was interrupted by the entrance of Gurth, closely followed by his faithful henchman Leofric.

"What! tears, Hilda?" exclaimed her brother, cheerily; "nay, nay, 'praying and working is better than crying,' I have heard thee say. I know little about the praying—that is for maiden folk, but 'tis better than crying, I ween. See, I have come to thee to buckle on my armour and send me forth to victory; and Gytha shall do the same for you, knave," pointing to Leofric.

Hilda dried her tears instantly, feeling half-ashamed that her brother had seen her betray such weakness. But when the last buckle was secured, and her brother bent to kiss her, the thought that she might never see that kindly handsome face again quite overcame her, and she clung to him for a moment, sobbing passionately, "Oh, Gurth, if I could go with thee!"

"Nay, nay, little sister, that cannot be; but 'twill help me in the battle to know thou art here and thinking of me—here, and not in the convent, Hilda; for thou wilt comfort my father and mother if—if I should not come back."

"I—I will pray for thee, Gurth; and Gytha shall take my last web of linen as an offering to the Church to speed thee in the battle," sobbed Hilda.

"Do as thou wilt about the linen so thou dost pray for me thyself, for I doubtless owe it somewhat to thy prayers that I have not run to the excess of riot I once did."

Hilda looked up through her tears and smiled. For Gurth to own so much was joyful news to his loving sister, and she ventured to whisper, "Wilt thou not pray for thyself, my brother?"

But he shook his head. "I am not fit, little sister; thou art my saint, and thou shalt do this for me."

"And dost thou think I am more fit of myself —fretful, unhappy that I have been? Nay, nay, Gurth, the Lord Christ, who alone could make me fit, will help thee an thou ask Him; fit to pray and fit to die," she whispered.

"Well, I will think of thy words, sister mine; but now I must say farewell;" and the next minute Gytha and Hilda were left alone, for the rest of the bower-maidens had gone to the yard to see the departure of fathers, and mothers, and friends as they rode away in the train of Godrith.

Most of them, like brave girls, had kept back their tears until the train of lithsmen and house-carles had gone, but they came back to their mistress' bower weeping bitterly, and for a little while Hilda could only weep in company. But she was the first to rouse herself and try to comfort them; and then she bade them spin and weave more industriously than ever, and sent Gytha to fetch all the clothes of the household that needed mending, for it was her duty now to see that her father's house-carles did not go ragged. She feared the campaign would be a long one; but in a few days came a messenger with the news that King Harold had fought and won a great battle at Stamford Bridge. Hilda had hardly received this news in her bower when another messenger arrived bringing tidings that William, Duke of the Normans, had landed on the shores of Sussex.

But this did not alarm the lady, as the landing of the Danes had done. "They are only Normans—a race of puny starvelings," she said contemptuously. "Bid them set a meal for the messengers, and see that others carry forward the tidings they bring, if they be wearied with their journey."

In a few days her mother, father, and brother arrived with the victorious army from York. Flushed with their recent victory over their most dreaded foes, they anticipated an easy victory over these Norman invaders; and, tired as they were by hasty marches, sang songs as they passed along the road, deriding Duke William's attempt to gain the crown of England.

Gurth and his father, with Leofric, could not stay more than an hour or two before they were obliged to journey on again. "My mother will not journey with us, Hilda, for she is already wearied; and 'twill be but a day or two, an thy saints help us, ere we return to celebrate another victory," said Gurth, showing her the silver baldric which the king had presented to him.

"But will not the king wait for reinforcements?" asked Hilda. "The King of Scots and the Northumbrians will surely give us succour."

"Nay, nay, we need it not," said Gurth, confidently; "with King Harold to lead us, victory were easy over any foe; and we will hold high wassail when we bid Duke William farewell."

"But this oath I have heard whispered about," said Hilda. "I am not fearful, Gurth, but 'twere well to make the victory sure; and is it wise

BALDRIC: *an ornamented belt worn over one shoulder to support a sword or bugle*
WASSAIL: *riotous drinking and carousing*

that the king should go to fight in the face of
this, even though it were extorted by Norman
guile?"

"Nay, nay, let not this trouble thee," said
Gurth, rather impatiently; "but tell me what I
shall bring thee from the spoil these proud Normans will leave behind."

He had heard others gravely discussing the
wisdom of the king leading his army in person
because of this oath, and because England would
lose all should any mischance befall the king.
But he had borne an almost charmed life hitherto,
and why should mischances befall him now?
asked Gurth almost fretfully, whenever he heard
any of these whispers from his friends; and he
could not help feeling impatient even with his
sister when she ventured to speak of caution too.

Droves of cattle and wagons full of barrels of
strong ale followed in the rear of the army, and
behind these went the women—the wives and
mothers, many of whom were already footsore
and weary with their long journey from York.

Hilda had by her own desire been carried out
in her litter to see her father and brother depart;
and when this train of weary, dusty, travel-
stained women came in sight her eyes filled with
tears.

"My mother, cannot we ask them to rest and
refresh themselves awhile?" she said. "Let some
bread and meat be brought out here, and a few

GUILE: *deception, cunning*

buckets of ale. I would I could journey on with them," she said; "but as this cannot be, I would fain help those who can."

A bountiful meal was soon spread on the grass inside the stockade, and the weary women invited to partake of it; and then, noticing that many of them looked poor and ragged, Hilda sent one of her bower-maidens to her store of clothes that had been prepared to give away to the poor, and distributed the garments to those who stood in most need of them. Then, more precious even than the clothes, she gave them some strips of linen fit to bind up wounds; for these brave-hearted women and a few monks were the only nurses and doctors who would go with the army to the battlefield, and it might be that a strip of linen would save a precious life.

So long as there were women to be fed and refreshed the feast on the grass was renewed, and many a stranger went on her toilsome journey strengthened by the food and cheered by the kindly hopeful words that Hilda contrived to speak to each as they passed her litter. To each and all it was much the same—God loved her and her dear ones at home and in the battlefield, and this world was only one step lower than heaven, where the saints beheld His face.

Perhaps the knowledge that Hilda, too, had a father and brother sharing the dangers that threatened their beloved ones added weight to her words of loving cheer; for the women talked of her and the wonderful words she had spoken all the rest of the journey, treasuring them in their minds to whisper in dying ears if no priest or monk should be near to give the last consolations of the Church.

Tired but hopeful Hilda went to her bower, but there was little spinning or sewing to be done now, for every few hours a messenger would pass to and from the army, and each must be questioned by the man posted at the drawbridge.

They heard at last that the two opposing armies had come face to face with each other, and that the Norman host was much more formidable than had been anticipated.

Early in the morning of the 14th of October a messenger rode past, saying a battle would be fought that day—had already begun. "We are not daunted by the number of our foes, but have held high wassail all night in honour of the victory we shall gain," he said, pausing for a moment to tell the news to the man at the postern.

All that day the battle raged, but towards evening came a messenger bringing the woeful tidings that the king was dead, and shortly afterwards came the inevitable news that Hilda knew must follow—the battle was lost—the king, his brothers, and the flower of his army had been slain.

POSTERN: *private back door or gate*

"Oh, my mother! my mother!" wailed Hilda, "this day thou wilt surely die."

"Nay, nay, it may be that thy father and brother have escaped," whispered Gytha, with white and trembling lips, thinking of her brother.

A little later and it was told Hilda that Leofric had arrived. "Then fetch him hither before he shall see my mother," commanded the lady, for she felt certain there was direful news to tell or Leofric would not come alone.

They brought him in as he was, hot, covered with dust, and stained with blood; but there was no time to question him as to his wounds—whether he was hurt.

"My master is safe, noble lady," he said quickly. "He hath bidden me ride on and tell thee he is trying to rally the men of Wessex to keep Duke William and his hosts at bay until wives and sisters have taken refuge in the convents. The Church alone can defend these now, and my master bade me tell ye all to go there," he said, looking round on the group of frightened bower-maidens, and speaking very bitterly.

"My brother, thou sayest, is safe, but, but—my father—what of him?" asked Hilda breathlessly.

Leofric turned aside, whispering to his sister, "Tell her—tell her he died a hero's death."

But Hilda heard the words, and partially raised herself on her couch. "And my mother! Think you she will go to the convent?" she asked.

"It is the only place for a lady now," said Leofric.

"It is no place for me now," said the lady; and to the astonishment of all present she struggled into a sitting posture, and gazed round upon her cowering bower-maidens with a look of such firm resolve that Leofric could almost fancy that the spirit of the dead knight lying on that fatal field of Senlac had that hour passed into his fragile invalid daughter.

"Come, maidens, and help me to dress; I must go to my mother," said Hilda.

But the girls could only stare at their mistress in blank amazement, for none of them had ever seen her help herself in this fashion before. In spite of the terror and anguish of that moment Hilda could not help smiling at her frightened maidens, and her newfound strength which their bewilderment had first made her aware of, for she had started from her pillow utterly unconscious of what she was doing. Gytha came towards her first, pale and frightened at the news she had heard, but smiling with joy at the wonderful improvement in her beloved mistress. She murmured something about this, but Hilda said hastily, "Never mind me, child; we must think of others now. Fasten my dress quickly, and let me go to my mother;" and, supported by two of her tallest girls, Hilda tottered to the great hall, where her mother sat fondling and petting her husband's dogs and favourite falcon, for none had ventured to tell her yet that Harold and England had fallen.

She started as she saw her daughter. "Hilda, Hilda, hath the wise woman cured thee at last?" she said; "this is joyful news, indeed, for thy father when he shall return;" and the stately lady led her daughter to her father's high-backed chair, where two hawks had perched themselves.

But at the mention of her father Hilda's courage almost gave way as she said, "Mother, Mother, hast thou not heard of the ill news, that the sacred banner of England is taken by William, Duke of the Normans?"

"The banner of Wessex! the royal dragon of King Edward! the symbol of England's rightful king! Child, child, King Harold would never part with that but with his life!" exclaimed her mother, starting from her seat as she spoke.

"It is gone," said Hilda mournfully.

"Then—then the battle is lost, not won," gasped Lady Elfrida.

"Leofric hath brought the news," said Hilda.

"Leofric, the churl! Where is my husband?— my son? Villain, where is thy master?" she said, turning fiercely upon Leofric, whom she now saw for the first time standing near the door.

Leofric dropped on one knee as the lady approached. "My master is fighting still—keeping

CHURL: *a rude, ill-bred person; from "ceorl" meaning peasant* the French at bay until ye have all taken refuge in the convents," he said.

"Taken refuge in the convents!" exclaimed the lady; "did my son dare to send such a message to me?"

"Alas! lady, until we can get help to drive the Normans back the Church alone can succour and aid the defenseless," said Leofric.

All the household had gathered in the great hall now—a frightened herd of women, girls, and boys, for all who could carry arms had followed their master to the fatal field of Senlac, and none had come back yet to tell how England's heroes had fought against overwhelming odds; and everyone standing there had seen some brother, husband, father, or friend go forth with their lord; and as they heard Leofric's words, one long, loud wail of anguish rang through the house.

"Hush, hush!" commanded Lady Elfrida; "this is no time for useless sorrow; if our menfolk are stricken down by the foe, women must arm for the fight;" and stern, tearless, and unwavering, she told Leofric to return to his master, and tell him that his mother was a Dane, and scorned the protection of Church or men while she could protect herself.

Chapter XIV

The Refuge

NGLAND lost! Who dares to utter
the coward thought?" exclaimed
Lady Elfrida when something like
calmness had been restored to her frightened
household.

Hilda was still sitting in her father's high-
backed chair, the hawks mounting guard, and
the bower-maidens gathered in a group round
her—most of them orphans now, for whom she
must think and care before she could think of
herself or even indulge her grief. There was no
time to be lost either. These must be provided
for; and then the remnant of their household
must retreat westward—away from the line of
march likely to be taken by the Normans should
they press on towards London.

"My mother, these must go to the convent,"
she said, looking round sadly at the frightened
weeping girls.

"I have nought to do with thy Church, Hilda;
I scorn her protection: but an thou wilt claim it

for thyself and thy maidens thou shalt not go empty-handed. There are silver cups enow for ye all, I trow," added the lady.

"Give them what ye will, my mother, but the convent is no place for me now that I can be helpful as another woman. I will go with thee to our old home near Winchester, but these shall go to the convent until—until—;" and there Hilda stopped, for there was no place for them in the world now except the convent, for if the Normans were driven out of England tomorrow it could not bring the dead back to life. So, turning to Gytha, she said:

"Thou wilt have thy wish at last. I will not keep thee from the convent now, Gytha, for I know not what perils and dangers may be before us."

"Perils and dangers for thee!" exclaimed Gytha. "Nay, nay, dear lady, thou dost need the protection of Holy Church as much as we thy poor maidens."

"Hush, hush, Gytha! God will protect me. The earth is still His footstool, I trow, though the Normans are in England."

"But thou art weak and frail; how canst thou brave dangers and perils?" protested Gytha.

"Because I cannot—will not—leave my mother and Gurth. But hasten now to the convent of St. Mary, and ask them to take thee and these poor maidens, and my mother will send all that can be spared as dowry with ye."

ENOW: *enough*
DOWRY: *a sum of money or its equivalent required for girls desiring to enter a convent*

At first the girls protested, that they would
not leave their mistress and had no wish to enter
the convent; and at last Hilda promised that if
she returned and was able to receive them she
would do so; but as most of them were very
young she could not take them with her now.

So an hour after Leofric's arrival Gytha set off
to the convent which she had so often longed to
enter. But as they drew near they saw that the
place was already besieged by eager applicants,
who claimed the protection of the Church not
only for themselves and their helpless little
children but for all they could carry of their
household possessions.

Father Alred stood at the gate, looking woe-
fully perplexed, but doing all he could to help
and encourage his frightened flock. He shook
his head sadly as Gytha drew near with the
group of girls. The convent was full, he said,
and he was obliged to refuse admission to these
poor women and children.

"Nay, nay, but thou hast long promised to
receive the Lady Hilda and me, her poor bower-
maiden, whenever we should desire to leave yon
godless household," said Gytha promptly.

"Holy father, we have no refuge but the convent now, for our fathers lie dead at Senlac," said
two of the girls, beginning to cry afresh as they
realized something of their desolation from the
frightened crowd standing round, who were so

unwilling to depart although they had been assured that St. Mary's could receive no more fugitives.

The monk looked pityingly at the two girls, but still shook his head. "Thou dost claim thy promised place here for thyself and the Lady Hilda?" he said, speaking to Gytha.

"Yes, yes," said Gytha, "I claim protection for two—myself and my lady-mistress—and will leave thee these two until we come ourselves;" and she pushed forward the two weeping girls, and, asking the nearest way to the next convent, prepared to turn away.

The monk looked puzzled, and felt he had been outwitted for once, but he could not turn away these two pretty, helpless girls. They were the youngest of Hilda's bower-maidens—little more than children, in fact, for they had not been with her long; but the fame of the Lady Hilda as a gentle, careful mistress made people anxious to send their daughters to her for the needful training in housewifely ways; and so these two had come when there were vacancies for fear they should not gain admission later. Having disposed of these two safely, Gytha hurried forward with the rest of her charge, fearing lest the next convent should also have been besieged, and trying to say a word of comfort to the poor girls as she went.

Leofric and other messengers had succeeded in

arousing the people to a sense of their danger, and every few yards they overtook a party of women and children hurrying forward in the same direction as themselves, or met groups of men who, having lodged their families in safety, were hastening to give what help they could to keep back the foe.

Everybody was anxious and fearful of the worst now, but the men looked resolute enough to dare anything, and Gytha began to hope that Lady Elfrida was right and England was not lost after all. But she hurried forward with none the less speed, but only to find that this convent, like the last, was already full.

On again she went, this time towards London, but it was not until she had grown footsore and weary that she had found a refuge for all Lady Hilda's bower-maidens. To each of them, as she bade them farewell, she whispered:

"Never forget thou hast a message to deliver —God's message of love to man. Our mistress bade me remind thee of this, and thou wilt not forget it for her sake."

"Where art thou going, Gytha?" asked the last as they stood at the convent gate, having with difficulty gained admission even for one here.

Gytha shook her head. "There is no room in the convent for me now, so I must even go back."

"Oh, Gytha, thou wilt be a slave again, and

thou wouldst be free in the convent! Let me go back, and do thou stay here."

"Nay, nay, I feel it not slavery to serve my noble mistress. It may be I should fail to serve God in the convent—I should miss serving the Lady Hilda so sorely."

"Gytha, thou wilt forgive me for all—all the unkind things I have done to thee," said the girl penitently.

"Nay, I have nought to forgive, child; but an thou dost think I have aught to pardon thou shalt—not earn it, mind, for it is thine already—but thou shalt pray for me because of thy recollection of this. The prayers of a holy nun thou knowest—"

"Nay, nay, call me not a holy nun," interrupted the girl with another burst of sobs; "thou art fit to be a nun, Gytha, and I would thou shouldst take this last chance and let me have the dangers there may be in the world."

But Gytha shook her head. "Better me than thee, child; I am almost a grown woman, and thou but a girl, and—and I am not sure about serving God in the convent with my noble lady mistress outside;" and so with another word of farewell Gytha saw her last companion enter the convent gates, and then slowly turned homewards. The shadows of evening were gathering before she reached home, and she was worn and weary with her long journey, but there was no time to rest. Her mistress was not greatly surprised to see her return, and received her with a look of glad welcome, but Lady Elfrida looked at her with stern displeasure. "I would fain have nought to do with the Church now," she said shortly.

"Nay, my mother, speak not unjustly to Gytha," said her daughter; "she hath ever served me faithfully, and I can but be thankful for any chance that doth send her back to me; and thou hast heard there was no room in the convent for her."

"She hath but come back to persuade thee to go," said her mother tartly.

Not yet had the stern self-contained lady allowed herself any indulgence to the grief she felt at the death of her lord. She had been busy all day issuing orders to the few house-carles to prepare for flight at once by packing all they could with them. She would have buried the most costly part of the treasure—the silver cups and jewel-hilted swords—but Hilda had at length succeeded in persuading her that it was only fair to send these to the convents that had sheltered her poor bower-maidens; and all the surplus of the harvest that they could not carry with them had been sent there too. But Lady Elfrida had given these things rather grudgingly; she had no more love for the Church than her husband or son, and she was often inclined to wish that Gurth had never bought these slaves at Bricstowe, for they had succeeded in keeping all priests and monks and all that they taught at a distance from Hilda until Gytha came.

The household was almost ready to start on the long journey to the half-ruinous farmhouse they had forsaken so many years ago, when Gytha reached home, and there was only time for her to snatch a hasty meal before her lady's litter was at the door.

Leofric had returned to tell his master what his mother had decided to do, and where she might be found. He did not venture to question the wisdom of the lady's plans openly, but he thought it was unwise to defer their departure until night, or having deferred it until then not to wait until the morning. National calamity was not likely to lessen the number of robbers or render them more considerate, but Lady Elfrida was not one likely to brook any advice from her house-carles, and so Leofric said nothing to them; but when he found his master he did not hesitate to tell him of his fears. But there was no time to think of this now. Gurth was one of a heroic band of free Wessex men, who had resolved to keep the foe at bay as long as possible, in the hope that succour might yet come from some quarter, and the hated Norman conqueror be driven back—back to his boats or into the sea; it mattered not which so that England was free.

BROOK: *stand for, tolerate*

But alas! alas! Harold was dead—the heart of England lay on that fatal field of Senlac, and though men were brave and performed prodigies of valour, they were but units. There was no leader who could turn this bravery to good account—no one to take the place of Harold the king, either as statesman or general; and at last the conviction was forced upon these heroic Wessex giants, and they gave up the unequal strife, lest there should not be a man left to help the good cause by and by, should hope dawn for them once more.

So Leofric and his master made their way to the new home about a week later, wounded, weak, and ill, and looking more like beggars than stalwart soldiers. They had no good news to bring. "Edgar the Ætheling hath been proclaimed king," said Gurth scornfully, "but 'tis a leader—one wise in counsel and skillful in war—that England needs now."

Lady Elfrida had showed herself a shrewd and wise woman in her choice of a refuge. They might have gone to their house at Charing, but that she deemed would be too great a prize to escape the grasp of the Normans if they succeeded in reaching London; but this farmhouse stood in the middle of a small island which was well-protected all round by high banks and a deep fringe of forest trees. The place had been neglected for years, but the fields could soon be brought under cultivation again, and with their reduced household they would be able to live in comparative comfort until brighter days dawned.

Gurth was told all this the moment he arrived, and he was thankful to see that his mother could take so much interest in all these details; but as soon as he could escape he made his way to the little lean-to which served as his sister's bower.

"Gurth, Gurth, thou hast come at last," said Hilda, tottering forward to meet her brother.

What with his surprise and what he had suffered from his wounds and want of food, Gurth almost fell to the ground at the sight of his stately sister walking to meet him.

"Hilda, Hilda, what is it?" he gasped.

"Did not Leofric tell thee of this change in my state?" she asked.

"Leofric! Did he know it then?"

"Yes, it was—oh, Gurth, it was when he brought the dreadful news that I sat up and walked to my mother."

"And thou hast walked ever since?"

"Yes, I walk a little every day leaning on Gytha's arm. But come now, we have talked enough of my poor self; let me tend thee. Have thy wounds been dressed at all?" she asked. "Thy shirt and tunic are full of rents and cuts, and stiff with blood, I can see."

"Yes, they are in ill condition, I trow; but the

sight of thee so brave and cheerful, and my mother so busy for thy sake, hath made me feel ashamed for my weakness and hopelessness. Thy God hath not forsaken thee, Hilda, and I would fain render Him some service for His goodness to thee. Come, let me see thee walk again before I go."

"Nay, nay, thou art not going yet. I will walk to yonder chest and get thee some clothes, and thou shalt change them here while I go to the kitchen and see to the stewing of some herbs I shall need for thy wounds. I can dress them for thee now, Gurth," she added proudly.

"So thou shalt, my lady sister; and I would that thy bower-maiden were here to do the same for my faithful knave, for there are none like women's fingers, I trow, for such work as this."

Hilda smiled. "And thou hast not heard that Gytha gave up her purpose of going to the convent?" she said.

"Nay, nay, I have heard nothing, it seems—nothing of the good news that was in store for me when I was half-inclined to turn robber, if I should find thee gone to the convent, as I feared thou hadst, in spite of what Leofric told me. Where is Gytha?" he asked quickly.

"With thy knave, her brother, I doubt not, since she hath not come back from the kitchen even to tell me of thy arrival;" and the next minute Gytha herself came into the room with a request for clothes and some linen bandages to bind her brother's wounds.

"See to it that he hath a plentiful supply of straw for his bed," said Gurth; "but he must drink sparingly of the strong ale, I trow, for we have eaten little these two days."

"And thou art hungry, my brother. Gytha, send one of the wenches hither with a trencher of bread and some of that cold beef, and a horn of water from the spring," said her mistress; "and thou mayst get the same for thy brother," she added.

Hilda went to look after the stewing of her herbs while Gurth changed his dirty ragged clothes, and when she came back and had dressed his wounds, and given him something to eat, the brother and sister began talking of the future; and Gurth said:

"Hilda, thy God hath been very good to thee —to thee and me too. I cannot serve Him as a monk, but I would fain serve Him as a Christian knight, an He will have me."

And Hilda kissed him and whispered, "He will receive and welcome thee, Gurth."

Chapter XV

The Two Knights

ADY ELFRIDA was profoundly astonished and greatly displeased when she
heard of Gurth's intention of being
knighted by a monk. She had not seen much of
her son since his return, for his wounds, long
neglected, required the more careful tendance
now, and he spent much of his time in his sister's
bower, where Hilda could bathe and dress them,
could read and talk to him, watch that he did
not drink too much strong ale to beguile the time,
and nurse him back to health and strength.

Coming into the bower one day from her task
of superintending some outdoor work, she startled
Hilda by suddenly snatching from her hand the
Book which she was reading to Gurth.

"Have I not said I will have nought to do with
the Church?" she said angrily.

"But, my mother, if the Church, or rather He
who is greater than the Church, even God himself,
had nought to do with us, we should be in sorry

case," said Hilda, gently looking towards her beloved Book, which her mother had thrown into the farthest corner of the room in her disgust.

The lady looked surprised and only half-pleased at her daughter's meekness. Hilda had shown such violent temper in bygone days, and she had been allowed to have so much her own way—so much more freedom than girls were usually allowed—that when the Book was snatched away Lady Elfrida was half-afraid of what she had done, and expected to see Hilda burst into a storm of passionate reproaches. But with the exception of a slight colour flushing her pale cheeks, and a little tremor about her mouth, there was nothing to show that Hilda felt the smallest rising of anger.

Gurth was almost as much astonished as his mother at his sister's patience. He had seen too little of the daily struggles, failures, and conquests that had finally given her this perfect mastery over her temper, but he understood it a little, which Lady Elfrida could not. She had not allowed her grief for her husband to have its way, but trampled it down with a stern, pitiless scorn, turning to the work of the farm—to provide a safe shelter for Hilda—as an outlet for her restless sorrow. She had looked upon Hilda's grief as a sign of weakness, and now her gentle patience was only a want of spirit in the eyes of her mother.

Gurth was by no means as patient as his sister, and took her part warmly, and in the midst of their quarrel announced his intention of being knighted by God's knights, the monks, which increased his mother's anger fourfold.

"It is well my Godrith hath departed to the halls of Valhalla. He died a hero's death, and will never know that his son covets to die like a cow in his bed, and hath struck hands with the Church in his craven fear."

"Nay, nay, my mother," said Hilda quickly, and flushing rosy red in her defense of her brother, "Gurth is no craven, no coward, and that thou knowest right well."

"No man ever called me coward," said Gurth, hoarse with rage, "and—and I should forget thou wert a woman if thou wert not my mother." And he towered above her, tall as she was, and looked as though he was about to shake her. He might have done even that in his mad rage, but an appealing glance from Hilda checked him, and he went and picked up her Book instead, and Lady Elfrida left the room.

"Hilda, I must seek these holy fathers at once, and they shall knight me, and Leofric too, an the fellow will," said Gurth as soon as his mother was gone.

"Be not too hasty, my brother; thou hast much to learn."

"Nay, nay, I have learned that God loves thee,

CRAVEN: *contemptibly faint-hearted*

GURTH AND LEOFRIC PREPARING FOR
KNIGHTHOOD

that He hath been good and kind and worked a miracle for thee, and it is enough. I will serve Him as I served King Harold. The world hath no second Harold, and I could not serve a less noble master than he now, and so I will strike hands with the King of kings, and be His servant."

Leofric, of course, would follow the example or do the bidding of his master, and so, as soon as their wounds were sufficiently healed, they went to a neighbouring convent where they knew that an English abbot ruled, and told him all their story, and asked to be made knights after the fashion of the Church.

Hilda would fain have had them both better instructed in the Christian faith, but Gurth would hear of no delay, since the abbot had not imposed any. His mother had called him "craven" and "coward," and he must prove at the sword's point that he was true son of Godrith, the brave, by joining the Londoners in their attempt to keep the conquerors at bay.

But a more severe test than any fighting was before these two candidates, and that was watching in the church all night. Gurth and his companion had not been in a church more than once or twice in their lives, and a feeling of awesome fear crept over them at the thought of kneeling in the dim light that gleamed from the altar all through the long hours of darkness. The priest

told them to think over their past lives, and con-
fess all their sins as they kneeled before God; and
there were plenty of youthful escapades that even
Gurth could not but own were far from innocent.
Then they were to look down into their hearts,
and see if they had courage to promise and vow
to live henceforth not to please themselves, but
to serve God in the defense of the weak, the poor,
and oppressed.

Gurth prayed to all the saints he had ever
heard of to help him through this ordeal, for
mental exertion was something to which he was
so entirely unused that he feared before half his
sins had been confessed he should be fast asleep.
He told his fears to Leofric, and, like a faithful
servant as he was, he promised to keep his master
from falling asleep; and he did it too, giving but
a divided attention to his own spiritual exercises
in watching and frequently rousing his master.

The long vigil came to an end at last. Before
day dawned the monks filed into church, and the
first service of the day commenced. High mass
would be performed later in the day, and Gurth
and Leofric would be knighted by the abbot immediately before this, so their patience was tried
a few hours longer. At last came the summons
for them to lay their swords on the altar, as laying down their own will and pleasure, and then
they knelt at the foot of the steps until the gospel
was read. The abbot then took the swords and

laid the blades on the bowed bare necks of the two candidates, bidding them take them and use them in the name of God and His apostles for the defense of the helpless and oppressed, the fatherless and widows, and God's servants the monks. Then they were girded once more with their weapons by the attendant monks, and went forth true and loyal knights to fight for home and fatherland, for the love of God who had shown such love to Hilda.

They were both very ignorant still. They did not know the names of half the saints in that Pantheon that had been thrust between God and men; and missing this, Gurth looked straight up to the God Hilda's Book told about, and vowed in heart and soul, as well as by word of mouth, to serve Him with his sword, and ever to help and succour the defenseless.

Leofric was no longer a slave even in name now. Gurth had freed him, but he had willingly given his hand to the Church, and now regarded himself as occupying a similar position towards God as he had formerly done towards his master, and the utmost of his service was due to Him now, as it had before been due to Gurth.

A few hours were spent at home, and then the two new-made knights rode forth to help the Londoners, and maintain the right of the young king to the crown of England. The news had already come that Duke William was bitterly

PANTHEON: *literally "temple of all gods"; refers to the mistaken belief that Christians must pray to God through the "saints"*

disappointed that the crown had not been offered
to him immediately after the death of Harold.
He wanted to claim it as his right by inheritance
and bequest, and dreaded and hated the name of
Conqueror. But as he was little likely to get it
in his own way, and was determined to have it,
force became necessary, and slowly he pushed on
his way to London, till more than one party of
Normans had been seen in the neighbourhood of
the little fortified farm.

This was growing to be a fortress and a refuge
for many a poor Saxon family who, driven from
their homes by the conquering Normans, were
glad to take refuge anywhere. Some of these
brought corn, and cattle, and household goods
with them, and only asked leave to build a hut
behind Lady Elfrida's well-planned defenses, but
others came ragged and famished with hunger;
but Hilda and Gurth had begged that all should
be admitted, and so Lady Elfrida received all,
although she gave the poorest but a sorry welcome. For the others she was rather glad of
their coming, since the men could help with the
defenses, while the women did the work of the
farm; and yielding deference to her she forgot
her grief and losses in the exercise of this new
power.

But if Lady Elfrida held the reins of authority,
it soon came to be known in the little community
that there was another whose influence was much

greater than that of the stern stately lady who went about the fields and outbuildings, and had such a sharp eye for detecting any delinquencies.

Lady Hilda's bower was still the center of this large motley household, and many a quarrel was pacified there that otherwise would have set them at war among themselves. There were none, perhaps, who worked harder than Hilda and Gytha now. Their distaffs and needles were always employed in providing clothes for the poor women and children, many of whom were almost naked when they came among them; and in the midst of these busy cares they almost forgot their own share in the terrible trouble that had befallen their beloved country.

The tales brought in by the fugitives of the cruelty and rapacity of their victorious foes made the heart grow sick, and after listening to a poor woman's account of how her husband had been murdered, and her home burnt before her eyes, Hilda exclaimed passionately, "Oh, Gytha, Gytha, surely God hath forgotten our poor England!"

Gytha could only shake her head and sob, for she was quite overcome at the heart-rending tale of distress, and she was wondering whether they would ever hear of the two young knights again, for several weeks had passed now, and nothing had been heard of them since their departure.

But private griefs and anxieties had to give way in the pressing need there was for somebody

RAPACITY: *greedy plundering*

to be peacemaker, comforter, and consoler, as well as provider for the material wants of those whom God had bereft of husbands and sons.

Lady Elfrida paid little heed to the ways of her household beyond seeing to its defenses and outside work, and very soon want began to make itself felt—a want, too, that these stalwart Saxons could ill brook. The store of ale came to an end, and men looked at each other wondering how they could live without strong ale, and a plentiful supply of it too.

Gytha carried the piteous tale to her mistress' bower with such a look of dismay on her face that the lady thought a troop of Normans had appeared.

"The ale all gone, Gytha!" she said with a short laugh; "then we shall have less quarreling, and the knaves will perforce learn temperance through the Normans after all."

But to Gytha it was no laughing matter. She recalled the scenes with her brother when he was sick and craved for this strong ale, and she feared that instead of less there would be more quarreling to settle now, and for a few days it seemed as though her fears were to be verified; for the men missed their accustomed potations, and grew cross and quarrelsome, and Hilda was appealed to again and again to settle the disputes that arose.

"Gytha, I feel worn out," said the lady one

PERFORCE: *be forced by circumstances*

evening. "These men and women know nothing of self-restraint or self-reliance; they are but little children, needing as much help, and guidance, and controlling. What will teach them to control themselves as men and women should?"

Gytha shook her head. She knew her mistress had been called upon to adjust one quarrel after another, and it was weariness now that made her feel so hopeless. "Nay, I know not what we can do more than we are doing for the poor knaves," she said; "but doubtless God can teach them all He will have them learn."

"Is it—is it that God would teach them this, that this sore trouble hath come upon our land?" she asked in an earnest whisper.

"Nay, I know not. Who can tell?" said Gytha with a deep-drawn sigh.

"But, Gytha, 'God is love,'" said her mistress. "Oh, if I could be sure about this—sure that it was to do these brave childish Saxons good that all these troubles have come upon us, then I think I could be content!"

"I too have sought to understand it; but when I listen to the tales about these cruel Normans, and how they are burning the happy homes of our Saxon England, I think all that the old monk of Bricstowe taught me must be a mistake."

"Nay, nay; but, Gytha, we have the Scriptures too. How many times have I read the very words thou didst bring as thy message to me."

"Then—then, is the Book wrong?" whispered Gytha.

"Nay, nay, I cannot bear to think that," said Hilda with a stifled sob; "for what should I do? what should I be if I could not believe that 'God is love,' Gytha? It must be that we cannot understand; we do not know all that God is doing, or we should be content."

"Content! when such cruelty and wrong are being done by our conquerors. Nay, nay, I cannot think God even would have us content," said Gytha hotly.

"Nay, I meant not that we should cease to help the oppressed as much as lieth in us. I would fain think that God hath given us this to do— this work of mercy—because He doth still love the people, though He chideth them right sorely, as a father doth a willful son whom he loveth."

"But what good can these evil-minded Normans do?" said Gytha petulantly.

"Nay, I know not, but thou must help me to believe still that this earth is God's footstool, Gytha, though the Normans be in our midst, and there is little hope now that they will be driven back very quickly. But here is my mother," added the lady hastily, and Gytha withdrew, making a lowly reverence to the elder lady as she passed.

Lady Elfrida looked troubled and anxious, and Hilda feared that some fresh calamity had be-

PETULANTLY: *irritably*

fallen them, for her mother seldom visited her bower now, except to bring some bad tidings or make some complaint. She seated herself as Gytha went out, and heaved a deep sigh. "Have they told thee the news?" she asked somewhat sternly.

"The news—of what, my mother? Hast thou news of Gurth at last?" she added hastily.

"Of him and of London too," said the lady bitterly; "such news as will make every English hero who fell at Senlac turn restlessly in his narrow bed—London is taken."

Hilda started from her seat with white face and clasped hands. "London hath been taken by the Normans!" she gasped.

"Ah, by the shaveling Norman; and he will have the crown too!" said Lady Elfrida.

"And Gurth, what of him?" asked his sister anxiously. "Hath he returned?"

A look of intense scorn passed over the lady's face as she answered, "Returned! nay, nay, he hath struck hands with the Conqueror, and will stay to feast with him in the halls of Harold and Edward. What have we here to offer in exchange for such a feast?"

"Nay, nay, my mother, thou knowest the Church is a haven and refuge in these evil times for all who are too weak to battle with the world's violence. But who brought tidings of Gurth?" she asked.

"A knave whom he sent with a message from our house at Charing, where he is abiding until this Duke William is crowned king of England."

Hilda looked puzzled. "May I see this same messenger, my mother?" she said.

"Yes, an thou wilt thou shalt see him, but he can tell thee little more than I have."

"Hast thou heard any more of the Normans thou didst see lingering about yesterday?"

"I have little fear of these pitiful shavelings," said the lady contemptuously, "they are too wise to attack us here, I trow; and when Gurth hath grown weary of his bondage to Duke William he can take refuge in our fortress."

Hilda would not notice this slighting speech concerning her brother, but she felt puzzled and anxious, and her interview with the messenger did not tend to lessen her perplexity. The man was not an actual idiot, but he was not much better, except in the matter of carrying a message which he learned to repeat parrot fashion, and to carry with the utmost speed. The message he had brought from Gurth was what Lady Elfrida had said. He had struck hands with Duke William, and would abide at Charing until after Yuletide, when he would be made King of England.

Had Gurth sent to say he was about to become a monk and retire to a monastery it would have surprised her far less than such news as this, but

after the first shock of surprise was over she resolved to wait before blaming him too much.
Something might happen to show her the heart
of this mystery by and by, and meanwhile she
would pray more earnestly than ever that her
brother might not forget his knightly vows.

Chapter XVI

Misunderstandings

N spite of Hilda's resolution to wait and pray and not judge Gurth too hardly, she could not help thinking bitterly of how his love of pleasure and good cheer had betrayed him into forgetfulness of his home and his knightly vows; for Yuletide came and passed, and the dreary winter settled down upon them, but no further message came from Gurth.

Lady Elfrida's outdoor employment was over now. The stockade and drawbridge over the little river had been made stout and strong, and the men could be trusted to keep up a constant watch at all points now that there was no ale or mead to rob them of their senses. But her work done, Lady Elfrida was seized with an illness, only too common in those days of undrained land. Ague was already making itself felt in their midst, among the women and children especially, but Lady Elfrida's seizure seemed to fill them with a sort of panic, for who would take the direction

AGUE: *a disease marked by fits of chills, fever and sweating; probably malaria*

of affairs now? Her daughter, the gentle Lady
Hilda, was too weak and delicate to leave the
shelter of her own bower and take the lead in
the great hall, and now everybody would be
striving for the master's seat at table.

Gytha heard something of these whisperings,
and carried them at once to her mistress. Hilda
was busy in attending to her mother, whom she
had persuaded to occupy her bower, as being the
most sheltered and comfortable room in the house.
But when the irritable old lady had been settled
on her daughter's bed, and she could leave her
for a few minutes, she went to discuss this fresh
difficulty with Gytha.

"The witless knaves will quarrel, thou sayest?"

"Ah, that will they, for who is to occupy the
master's seat among them where all are masters?"
said Gytha.

"I will—I must," said Hilda decisively, though
what it would cost her to give up the quiet retirement of her own bower at mealtimes not
even Gytha knew. As Lady Elfrida once said,
Hilda's affliction had made her fastidious, and
the faint smell of rotting rushes, dirt, and scraps
left from the table in various stages of putrefaction, was to her unaccustomed senses simply dis-
gusting. But she determined to endure this for
the sake of maintaining peace and order in their
large and motley household. And so, when the
dinner was ready, to the surprise of all present,

PUTREFACTION: *rotting*

Hilda, attended by her solitary bower-maiden to stand behind her chair, took her place where her mother usually sat, and every murmur of sedition and discontent was quelled; for no one wished to question the gentle Lady Hilda's right to rule them, even if they could have done so.

The servitors brought in the meat on spits, but Hilda could scarcely touch a morsel, her thoughts being all of her brother, and how he was wasting his time, feasting at the table of their common foe, instead of taking his rightful place at the head of his father's household.

Think of it as she would, Hilda could no longer find any excuse for her brother's absence; for they knew now all too well that half of England, at least, was conquered and lay passive at the feet of the Normans, unless it were a few isolated spots like their own home, which Hilda began to suspect was too insignificant to be attacked, as they had at first feared.

This taking her mother's place as the head of the household became a daily trial to Hilda, but she bore it without a murmur for the sake of those she ruled over, and often cheered her mother's lonely hours by an account of what passed during mealtimes.

It was a sad, gloomy, monotonous winter for all, and the men, deprived of their usual solacement of ale and mead, and a good deal of the rough outdoor amusement besides, grew fretful

SEDITION: *rebellion*
QUELLED: *quieted*

and discontented, and talked of leaving their safe quarters and taking their chance of an encounter with their foes outside. Parties of Norman soldiery were frequently seen patrolling the neighbourhood; but although they frequently paused to look at the island-fastness, they never molested the sentinels posted on duty by even a chance arrow. Hilda often wondered, and thanked God as she did so, for this clemency of their foes towards them; for tales of horror often reached them of what was going on outside. She could not think, as her mother did, that the enemy was afraid to attack them, but in what lay the secret of their safety she did not know. So the winter wore away, and with the first days of March came the knights Gurth and Leofric.

The brother and sister met as they had never met before—a coldness and suspicion had arisen between them. Hilda would not ask her brother for an explanation of his long absence, or what he had been doing at the court of the Norman king—made no reference to his knightly vows, or how she feared he had been living in violation of them, but simply talked of everyday topics and the news he brought from London. All unwittingly Gurth gave the deepest offense by telling this news, for he could not but own that William was a brave knight, and he had promised to rule his new subjects by their own Saxon laws, had confirmed the charter with all its privileges

CLEMENCY: *mercy*

to the city of London, and was striving to increase its trade and introduce learning and improvements in buildings and native manufactures.

"And will these things rear ruined homes and build the towns he hath burned?" asked Hilda indignantly.

"Nay, nay, I said not that it would; but thou didst tell me once to be just even to our foes, and as thou hast heard so much ill of the Normans, it is but fair thou shouldst know what there is of good in their doings."

"It is little enough, I ween—little beyond Norman guile to make Englishmen forget their homes and their wrongs," said Hilda indignantly.

"Nay, nay, my sister, thou art unjust to—"

"Unjust to thy new friends," interrupted Hilda passionately. "An thou hadst been here instead of holding high wassail with the Conqueror, thou wouldst have a better idea of justice."

"Nay, nay, but thou art unjust to me, Hilda," said Gurth; and there he stopped.

His sister looked at him as if hoping, longing to hear him say something that would justify his late conduct—that would clear up something of the mystery in which it seemed to be shrouded; but when he paused she rose from her seat, drew herself up to her full height, and in a voice of scornful contempt exclaimed: "Unjust to thee, Gurth Godrithson—nay, nay, that were impossible, thou recreant knight and God-forgetting Englishman."

"Hilda, Hilda, thou art cruel and unjust. If thou didst know all—"

"Then why not tell me? Nay, nay, what am I saying? I scorn to listen to thy tale of abject servility. Thou art no longer brother of mine, for I am English and the daughter of a hero, but thou—thou art what my mother called thee;" and without another word Hilda left the great hall where they had met and went to her own bower.

Hilda did not believe her brother would go away without giving some explanation of his conduct. She felt bitterly disappointed in him, yet still had clung to the hope that there might be some excuse after all. But if there was, would he not at once have urged it? and would she not have been too ready to make allowance for temptation? Now, when she heard that he had gone, leaving only a message for Leofric to follow him, she felt that all hope was at an end–that the brother she had loved so devotedly was dead to all honour, and she would rather he had fallen at the fatal field of Senlac than live to bring disgrace on the name of Englishman.

For her mother's sake she tried to hide her grief, but the old lady had grown watchful of her daughter's countenance, and very soon detected the signs of emotion.

RECREANT: *cowardly, deserting*
ABJECT: *miserable, wretched*

"Hilda, thou art hiding something from me," she said sharply.

"My mother," said Hilda, and there she stopped.

"Yes, I am thy mother, and live but for thee, Hilda; for if thou hadst gone to the convent I would have been true Danish wife to my lord, and speedily joined him in the halls of Valhalla; but thou wert his child and a brave true English-woman, and I could not but live to protect thy weakness and provide thee with a home."

"And it hath been a home and refuge to many others besides, my mother," said Hilda, anxious to turn the conversation.

"Yes, it hath, but it is not that troubles thee now, I ween. Thou art troubled, Hilda. Hath any tidings come of Gurth?" suddenly asked her mother.

"Yes," answered Hilda slowly, "he—he hath been here."

"Been here! But he hath not gone without saying a word to me!" exclaimed Lady Elfrida excitedly.

"I—I know not whether he will come back," said Hilda, scarcely able to restrain her tears as she spoke.

"Thou hast quarreled with him, Hilda," said her mother in an injured tone. "Oh, why did he not come to me before he went! Gurth, Gurth, I am thy mother!" said the old lady passionately, and then she reproached Hilda bitterly for her hardness and cruelty in driving her brother away.

Poor Hilda had enough to bear just now, and scarce knowing what she said she exclaimed in her passion, "Nay, nay, call me not hard and cruel, for he is more Norman than Duke William himself, I ween, or he would never—"

"And what care I?" screamed Lady Elfrida; "English or Norman, he is my son. I am his mother, and mothers are more tender than sisters. Oh, Gurth! why didst thou not come to me?" she sobbed.

"My mother, he shall come," said Hilda very calmly, but at the same time feeling very anxious, for what could this change in her mother portend? She had never seen her in this mood before, and had failed to notice the gradual softening that had been going on during her mother's illness.

"Thou dost blame my poor Gurth for what is thine own doing," said Lady Elfrida fretfully. "Nothing would content thee but he should be a knight of the Church's making; and now he hath learned the lesson she doth teach, to bow to the will of the strongest, thou dost blame him. Oh, Gurth, Gurth! thou hast been robbed of valour and honour and all that an Englishman holds dear, by becoming the slave of the Church."

Hilda felt vexed at her mother's inconsistent defense of her brother, and she knew it would be worse than useless to contradict it; but it re-

PORTEND: *foretell*

quired no small amount of patience to listen quietly to her mother's angry tirades against the Church, which she blamed as the sole cause of all her son's recent shortcomings and misdoings.

Hilda was very thankful when Gytha came to summon her to supper. She had not seen her bower-maiden since the arrival of her brother in the morning, for Gytha had spent the day with Leofric, and had heard a good deal more about their life at court than had her mistress. And Hilda, half-hoping to see her brother in the great hall, glanced down the long table set for the servants and retainers, but was disappointed to notice that Leofric was not among them.

"Where is thy brother, Gytha?" she whispered as the servitors were bringing in the spits.

"He hath gone to meet Sir Gurth on the road to Dover."

"To Dover! And wherefore doth he journey to Dover?" asked Hilda.

It was Gytha's turn to be astonished now. "Didst thou not hear that William the king hath commanded them and many other noble Saxons to go in his train to his court of Rouen?"

Hilda shook her head. "Thou shalt tell me of this and all thou hast heard from Leofric when supper is at an end," she said; but she felt even more bitter towards her brother as she thought of him hurrying away to join in the gaieties of the court of Normandy.

The quiet talk Hilda longed to have with her faithful bower-maiden had to be deferred until Lady Elfrida was fast asleep, and then mistress and maid drew close together and talked in subdued whispers by the embers of the logs still burning in the middle of the room.

"They are right noble knights," began Gytha, the tears glistening in her eyes as she spoke.

"Noble knights!" repeated Hilda; "nay, they have forgotten all their knightly vows. Oh, Gytha, they swore to be God's knights too!" added the lady sorrowfully.

"And are they not God's knights? Have they not given up their own wishes and desires, even liberty itself, to save us?"

"What dost thou mean? Who art thou talking of, Gytha?" asked her mistress.

"Of Sir Gurth and my brother; they are right noble Christian knights," said Gytha, in a tone of admiration.

"Why, who hath told thee this?"

"Who could tell me but Leofric, noble lady?"

"And thou didst believe him because he said, 'We are true knights'?" asked Hilda.

"Nay, Leofric said nought concerning that; he did but tell me how he and Sir Gurth had laid down their swords at the bidding of good Bishop Aldred."

"Then my mother was right, and it was done at the bidding of the Church," said Hilda hotly.

"Yes, and to save us from sharing the fate of so many others. We should have been murdered, and this house burned, but for the patience and forbearance of Sir Gurth, and the intercession of Bishop Aldred, who went unto the king and begged him to grant Sir Gurth his father's lands in these parts. The king did not yield very readily; and only on condition that Sir Gurth stayed near the court, and went with him when he went to Normandy, did he grant the petition of the good bishop on our behalf."

"Who told thee all this, Gytha?" asked Hilda in a troubled voice.

"My brother. I chided him at first for feasting in the halls of the Norman king, while we were often in sore dismay here and needed the help of good swords; and then he told me his master had given us more effectual help by not using the sword, but giving himself a prisoner for us."

"My brother a prisoner! Gurth gave up the dearest heritage of an Englishman, his liberty, to save us!" exclaimed Hilda, and then she burst into a violent flood of tears.

"Nay, nay, weep not so, dear lady. Perhaps I ought not to have told thee, for Leofric said his master would not have thee know he was a prisoner, lest thou shouldst grieve too sorely for him."

"Oh! would that I had known this before. Gytha, Gytha, I met my brother with reproaches and chided him as a recreant knight, who had forgotten his new-made vows, thinking of nought but his own pleasure. Oh! would that I had known; but now it is too late—too late."

"And did ye part from Sir Gurth in anger?" asked Gytha sadly.

"In anger!—Gytha, I must have been mad, or I could not have said what I did in my passion. Oh, Gurth, Gurth, how deeply have I wronged thee, charging thee with foulest wrong when thou hadst proved thyself a peerless Christian knight! Oh, Gurth, Gurth!" and the lady rocked herself to and fro, wailing forth her brother's name, and imploring him to come back, until at last Gytha became seriously alarmed.

At length, however, this passionate outburst of sorrow somewhat subsided, and she allowed Gytha to help her get into bed; but long after all other sounds in the house were still, a smothered sob from Hilda told that she was not asleep.

PEERLESS: *matchless, beyond comparison*

Chapter XVII

Sir Gurth

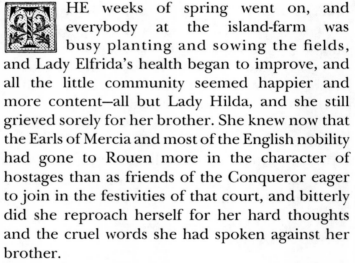HE weeks of spring went on, and everybody at the island-farm was busy planting and sowing the fields, and Lady Elfrida's health began to improve, and all the little community seemed happier and more content—all but Lady Hilda, and she still grieved sorely for her brother. She knew now that the Earls of Mercia and most of the English nobility had gone to Rouen more in the character of hostages than as friends of the Conqueror eager to join in the festivities of that court, and bitterly did she reproach herself for her hard thoughts and the cruel words she had spoken against her brother.

Those were not the days of letter writing, and since Gurth rode away smarting under her unjust suspicions, no word had come from him or Leofric, and so Hilda could not even have the satisfaction of letting him know that her opinion had changed, or of hearing that he had forgiven her.

One day, when she was sitting in her bower busy with her embroidery, she suddenly said to Gytha, "Was ever one more cruelly, more unjustly suspected than my noble Gurth? Hast thou heard of the fresh cruelties of this Norman bishop, whom the king hath left to govern in his stead? Ah, Gytha, we little know how we are indebted to our noble knights for permission to live here in peace—what it cost them—brave, valorous souls, ever ready to draw sword or bow to avenge a quarrel—what it was to them to lay these aside when burning to use them, and be peaceable and strike hands with the Conqueror—give up even liberty itself to buy this refuge for us poor helpless women; for even God hath forgotten our merrie England now!" added the lady bitterly.

"Nay, nay, the earth is God's footstool, although the Norman hath laid waste our land. May it not be that thou art judging God now as hardly and unjustly as thou didst thy brother awhile since, because thou dost not understand His work?" said Gytha.

"Nay, but are we not taught that 'God is love'? and can it be love to permit such evil doings as have desolated our merrie England?" demanded Hilda.

"But may it not be that God would fain do us some good—make our country greater, better—teach us things we would not learn in any other

VALOROUS: *courageous*

way than through force? Leofric brought this to my mind when he came; for when I grieved at all the hard things the Normans had done, he said, 'May it not be that God is treating our England as thou didst me when I was sick, giving me bitter potions, and denying me what I most craved, because thou didst love me? Did not the monk tell me I was worth saving, and so he made his potions the more bitter?'"

"Did the knave say that, Gytha? Nay, but how could he comfort himself with that thought?" said the lady.

"I know not that it did comfort him much, but he said it to comfort me, and I have thought of it often since."

"But thy brother was sick when thou didst give him these bitter potions," said Hilda.

"And I have heard thee say that many things needed amending in this our England—that men should exercise temperance and learn self-control, and cultivate learning, and have more cleanly ways in the matter of changing rushes, and other things that make life pleasant."

"And thou thinkest they may learn these of our Norman foes?" asked her mistress incredulously.

"It may be so; at least we may believe that God hath some good in store. It were better to hope this than fret ourselves by mistrustful thoughts, as thou didst concerning Sir Gurth and his tarrying at the court of the Norman."

"Ah, if I had but known—if I had only understood what my brother was doing for us!" said
Hilda with a sigh.

"And can we understand God better than we
could Sir Gurth?" asked Gytha. "I have heard
thee say that thou wert most blameworthy that
thou didst think evil of thy brother because thou
hadst always known him to be true and brave
and loving to thee; and shall we not trust God
now, though we may not understand Him, because
of the love He hath shown towards us—loving
us even to the giving up of His dear Son to die
for us?"

"Oh, Gytha, if I could only believe this again,"
said Hilda, with a deep-drawn sigh.

"Nay, but thou dost believe that the Lord
Christ hath died to redeem us, out of the great
love He doth bear us."

"Yes, yes, I must, I do believe that," said
Hilda.

"Then if God hath given His most precious
gift—His dear Son—will He withhold the lesser
gifts—peace, and comfort, and security? unless
He seeth that we must needs lose these for
awhile to make room for a greater good He hath
in store for us."

In this way did Gytha try to comfort her mistress, and to assure herself. Still it was hard to
believe that God had not forgotten them and
their beloved land, when every stranger who

came that way brought some fresh tale of Norman avarice and cruelty.

Then came rumours of the people rising to throw off the yoke of the Conqueror; and Hilda's cheek glowed and her breath came fast as she said, "The hearts of Englishmen are not crushed; we shall be English still, and the Normans must fly beyond the seas or be swallowed up by us. Mother, Mother, England is not dead; God will not let her die," she added, as Lady Elfrida came into her bower.

"Hush, hush, Hilda! thou must be heedful what thou sayest. The witless knaves are ready for any wild deed."

"It is for home and fatherland they would strike," said Hilda proudly.

"Yes, thou sayest truly; and if—if they had a leader, and could unite in one great rising, there would be hope, but not now—not a handful of men here and there; it is but throwing away brave lives, and making more widows and orphans, with fewer to work for them."

Hilda looked surprised to hear her mother speak thus cautiously. "Nay, but if we could throw off the Norman yoke, my mother," she began.

"And dost thou forget that the Normans hold thy brother, my son, my beloved Gurth, as hostage for our peace? I tell thee, Hilda, this is a refuge for the helpless—for women and children,

AVARICE: *greed*

and those who cannot defend themselves, but not a camp or a fortress; and those who will fain throw their lives away must e'en leave us first."

"Pardon me, my mother. I had forgotten that we held this land for Gurth, and that his life may be forfeit if we make it other than what he pleaded it should be—a refuge for the homeless."

It was well that Lady Elfrida did act with this prudent discretion, and discourage any of her followers taking up arms against their foes, for Norman troops in the neighbourhood watched them narrowly all through the summer, and would have been only too glad of an excuse for turning them out of their stronghold and appropriating it to themselves; but it was whispered that Sir Gurth stood so high in the king's favour, that so long as his mother and sister merely fed and clothed and lodged their starving country-folk, there was no hope of dispossessing them.

So the summer passed, and during the autumn came the news that before the close of the year King William might be expected to return to England; and from that time Hilda became more hopeful and cheerful. For some months her health had not been quite so good, and she rarely left her couch; but now the hope of seeing her beloved brother seemed to give her renewed strength, and she once more went about, leaning on Gytha's arm, and talking of the time when her brother would be with them once more, and all misunderstanding at an end.

"Oh, Gytha, I have grieved him so sorely, so needlessly! can it be, think you, that God is thus grieved when we mistake what He is doing for us, and complain and murmur, as I have often done of late? Oh, Gytha, if it should be that God is helping England in the only way, the best way, He can, just as Gurth was helping us when we thought he had forgotten us, how angry He must be at our murmurings!"

"Nay, nay, not angry, because He doth know us altogether. Doubtless it grieveth Him that those who have heard and learned His message of love will not believe it, because they cannot understand His work; but He is sorry for them most because they are fretful and uneasy, and it hinders them in what they might do for Him— do to help others, I mean."

"Ah, I have done little of late but lament for Gurth, and what God is doing for our merrie England, but I will try to believe once more that 'God is love.'"

The news that Sir Gurth was coming home from Normandy soon spread through the little community, and a few of the men who knew him resolved to go and meet him on the road, to tell him that his mother and sister desired to see him, and Hilda was only too glad to second their project, for she knew not whether her brother would come to them or journey on direct to London, unless she could send him some token of the change in her opinions.

Hilda grew almost weary of waiting, but her brother came at last—a grave, dignified, rather sad-looking man, not at all like the merry-hearted Gurth of the olden days. The change struck his sister painfully, and she burst into tears, sobbing, "Oh, Gurth, my brother, canst thou ever forgive me?"

"Forgive thee, little sister! nay, nay, I have nought to forgive, but much to bless thee for, Hilda," said Gurth, kissing her as tenderly as he used in his boyish days.

"Oh, Gurth, I have been cruel and unjust in my thoughts of thee," said Hilda.

"Ah, thou didst not know all, and I comforted myself with this thought, though it pained me that thou shouldst think I had broken my knightly vows. It would have pleased thee, and more than pleased me, to wield sword and battle-axe against the Conqueror, but Bishop Aldred taught me that for thy sake and the poor women-folk and helpless house-carles thou hadst sheltered, and whose champion and protector I had sworn to be, it were better to conquer myself first, and then strike hands with Duke William to hold my father's land in peace."

"Yes, yes; and while thou wert conquering thyself, as true Christian knight, to help us more effectually, I was blaming thee as though thou hadst forsaken us."

"But thou wilt not blame me again, little sister; and now let us talk of other matters. I have seen my mother in the great hall; what hast thou been doing to her, Hilda? she is greatly changed, I ween."

"Not as much as thou art, I trow," said his sister, looking up into his serious face.

"Not more, perhaps; for I have learned many things at Rouen I never heard of before. Didst thou ever think, Hilda, that there could be a power in the world greater than sword or battle-axe?"

"Nay, nay, the strong and the valiant will ever rule the world, Gurth," she said.

But her brother shook his head. "It hath been so, I ween; but there is another force rising now that shall be stronger than the arms of the mighty. There is a little priest at Rouen, one Lanfranc, that is proving this to the world, that learning and wisdom—the power of the mind— shall one day be stronger than force of battle-axe."

But Hilda looked incredulous. "Is this what thou hast learned of these guileful Normans?" she said, rather pettishly.

"The Normans have opened mine eyes, Hilda; but I think I have been learning this of thee, little sister, for many years."

"Of me!" exclaimed the lady in surprise.

Her brother smiled at her astonishment. "Was not thy bower the heart of the household in the old days, even as it is now, I doubt not?" he said.

"Nay, but I am not learned," said Hilda.

"But thou dost possess what takes the place of learning to those who love thee. Thou hast not strength of arms that all men have worshiped, but thou didst rule my life by another and a stronger power; and it is this that we have been learning in our home that the world will learn now, and our merrie England too, I trow, now that the Normans have possession of it."

"Gurth, thou dost not hate the Normans as I do—as thou wilt when thou dost know them better," said Hilda.

Her brother smiled. "Dost thou think I have been to the court of Rouen and learned nothing of their cunning and their cruelty, their pride and their greed? Nay, nay, I know more of these things than thou canst tell me, and yet I say, as thou told me once, if we will only learn some things these Frenchmen can teach us, and profit by the improvements they will bring with them, their coming to England may not be the bitter curse we now think it."

"Gytha hath said something like this, and I may hope it by and by, but not yet—not yet," said Hilda sadly.

"Wait till thou hast seen the gracious and noble Lady Matilda—Hilda; she is to be called the Queen of England, not the Lady of England, and she will be the first queen. She hath her court at Rouen, and hath much power in influencing her lord; so thou seest that what thou hast been doing, Hilda, in our home will be the fashion soon in all homes, although it seemed so strange and unlikely but a short while since."

"And this Lady Matilda, what is she like, and when doth she purpose to come to England?" asked Hilda.

"She is beautiful and a right gracious lady, and doth hope to see her new subjects in the spring. She is deft as thyself in the use of the needle too; her maidens are ever spinning or working in gorgeous silks at some tapestry. She hath done much for her city of Rouen, bringing with her from Flanders workmen who can weave and masons that can build better than any others in the world."

"And thou thinkest she will bring these same workmen with her to England?" said Hilda, trying to appear interested in her brother's account of their queen; but she would far rather have heard of some Danish sea-king coming to help them to drive the Normans out, for the Danes were in some sort their kinsfolk after all, and if they did bring little but devastation and barbarism, still Hilda was disposed to think that this even was preferable to what they were suffering under Norman domination.

As Gurth had said, his mother was changed. She was more gentle and affectionate than he had ever known her before. The weeks spent in Hilda's bower had softened the stern old lady. Even her hatred of the Church seemed to be forgotten; and to Gurth's amazement he found her sitting one day in his sister's bower listening as Hilda read from the Book he had bought, and afterwards she would even teach the children King Alfred's "dooms," as the Ten Commandments were then called.

But in spite of these changes in his mother Gurth went to London feeling anything but comfortable at the state of things in his island-home, for Hilda seemed restless, dissatisfied, and unhappy, and he feared that this feeling might spread in the little community until they were drawn into the commission of some rash deed that would bring destruction upon the refuge that had sheltered so many helpless men and women.

Chapter XVIII

Conclusion

SPRING sunshine again gladdened all the earth, and something like gladness shone in the faces of the eager crowd thronging the streets of Winchester anxious to catch a glimpse of the lady who was about to be proclaimed the Queen of England.

At a window of one of the houses near the palace sat our old friends Gurth and Hilda watching the crowd below.

"I am so glad, so thankful," whispered Hilda as the sounds of laughing and jesting were heard.

"Thou art less unhappy, I can see, little sister. I have lived in dread all the winter lest thou shouldst set the witless knaves to revolt against King William."

His sister lifted her eyes and looked at her brother in astonishment. "Why didst thou fear that?" she asked.

"Because when I came home from Rouen I

found thee restless and unhappy—so unhappy that thou didst think God had forgotten our merrie England, and thou wert ready to do anything to remedy this thyself."

"But what could I do—I who can scarce lift a battle-axe an inch from the ground?" exclaimed Hilda.

"Nay; did I not tell thee there is another power at work in the world now? It may be it hath ever been here, only buried in the convents and monasteries, as thine would have been an thou hadst had thy will and gone thither to become a saint. Hast thou ever thought, Hilda, that but for thy giving up this plan there would be no refuge here for the helpless women and children, and they must have perished long ere this?"

"Nay, but thou dost hold this land, Gurth," said his sister.

"Ah! in faith of being a Christian knight. But dost thou think I should have been a knight, or even worthy to have served our right noble King Harold, but for thee, Hilda? I tell thee, little sister, if thou hadst not been in thy bower when I came home after being condemned at Earl Harold's folk-mote, witless and wild should I have been even to this day had I lived so long. Now dost thou understand what I dreaded when I left thee last winter?"

FOLK-MOTE: *a general assembly of the people in early England*

But Hilda shook her head. "I knew not that thou didst dread anything," she said.

"It was this power thou hast to influence all who know thee. Thou wert unhappy—could not believe any longer thy favourite word that 'God is love' for our merrie England; and I feared the witless knaves would catch something of thy restless dissatisfaction and do some rash deed, instead of abiding in peace for the sake of the womenfolk and helpless children."

"And thou didst fear this—nay, it must have been told thee, for it was what did happen, and my mother had much ado to keep them from giving battle to the Norman troops when they passed. I besought them to remember that it was a refuge for those who had no other home and that God had not forsaken them; and somehow in talking to them I grew to hope and believe it myself—to believe that though we were under the cloud and could see no light, still the sun would shine again; that God still loved us though our portion was bitter just now; and I told them about Leofric's illness and what he had said about it, until at last they agreed to hang up the arms they had taken down to furbish, and I went back to my bower to thank God and remember that He did love us after all, and I have never doubted it since."

There was no time to say more, for the loud

shouts of the people gave them warning that the cavalcade of the queen was approaching; and a few minutes afterwards the beautiful stately wife of the Conqueror rode past, closely followed by the young princes and princesses, who looked half-pleased, half-frightened at the tumultuous reception that was given them.

"Gurth, Gurth, she is more Saxon than Norman," whispered Hilda excitedly as Matilda passed.

"Didst thou not know that she is a descendant of our own King Alfred?" said her brother. "King William doth often mention this as giving him a right to the crown, as well as his boasted promise received from King Edward. Nothing offends him more than to hear himself spoken of as 'the Conqueror.' He will never own he hath won the kingdom by conquest."

"I shall always call him 'the Conqueror,' much as I hate to be reminded of our defeat at Senlac," whispered Hilda. "But, Gurth," she went on, "I can love this Lady Matilda though I may hate her lord."

"Thou shalt have an opportunity ere long of seeing more of our new queen. I have already been bidden to take thee to the palace, for the fame of the work wrought by the Saxon ladies hath already reached her ears, and she doth desire to show thee something she and her ladies are now working as a present for her lord. It may be she will ask thee to stay awhile and help her with this same work," added Gurth gently.

"I will not promise to do that," said Hilda quickly.

"Nay, but thou must be cautious, Hilda. Thou must not forget it is by grace of this lady's lord that I hold this refuge which thou sayest hath given shelter to so many who have no other home."

"But, my brother," Hilda began. She did not say anymore, for a look of such bitter pain crossed his face, and he whispered hoarsely, "It may be we shall yet be free. I may yet be able to use my sword to help the oppressed without its being a signal for their slaughter, but until then I must remember my knightly vows, and thou wilt not forget thou art my sister."

Hilda understood her brother's meaning; and when a few days afterwards she went to the queen's bower to be presented to her and her ladies, and was invited to take a needle and show her skill in its use, she remembered her brother's words and at once assented.

But who shall describe her feelings when the portion that was already worked was uncovered? "That is the royal standard of England," she exclaimed, as this first met her view. Another look and she became convinced that it was the fatal

HILDA'S INTERVIEW WITH QUEEN MATILDA

field of Senlac where her father and so many of her noble countrymen fell, that was being depicted in these bright-coloured silks.

"Is it not a right noble work?" asked one of the ladies, covering up the finished portion and showing her some that as yet had only been painted in readiness for them to work. The canvas was about nine inches wide, but was expected to be sixty or seventy yards in length by the time it was completed. A dwarf sat before a table at one end of the room painting more canvas in readiness for the ladies' needles, but it all related to the same subject—the conquest of England.

Hilda took her needle and sat down, thankful that she had to work at some trees, and not the hateful figure of the Conqueror himself; but still it was very hard, very bitter to have to do this work, and nothing but the thought of those who might be turned out to perish from want, or as the prey of the Norman troops, enabled her to subdue the proud rebellious feeling that rose in her heart against it.

She soon found that she was not the only Saxon lady to be employed at this famous embroidery. Others were pressed into the service; and it became evident that kind and anxious as Matilda was to benefit her new subjects as a queen, she must not be offended as a woman, or trouble would fall upon the offender. This famous tapestry work, that was to commemorate the achievement of her husband, occupied so much of her time and attention, and she was so glad of any help she could get towards its completion, that Hilda knew most of the time spent at Winchester would have to be given to the queen and her work. But then, while she was here Gurth was free to leave the court and attend to his own concerns on the farm, and he and Leofric went and came between London and Winchester at their own will, eager, however, and anxious for any news from the north; for the Earls of Mercia and Northumbria had raised the standard of revolt, and Gurth would gladly have given them the help of his strong arm but for those who would have suffered so sorely through it. His mother and sister—to say nothing of those poor creatures who, driven from their homes, had no shelter but such as his lands afforded them—these must be protected and shielded, though what it cost Gurth to remain quiet at this time no one knew. He could only live in hope that the time would come when he might use sword and battle-axe to some advantage, but it was useless to stir up rebellion now, for they had not the smallest chance against the well-disciplined Norman troops.

These hopes, however, he confided to no one but his faithful follower Leofric. To his mother

and sister he always spoke hopefully and en-
couragingly, and there certainly was hope that
William would govern according to their own
Saxon laws. Gurth wished he could believe as
Hilda did—resting and working in the faith that
God was overruling all these calamities; for he
could see that it not only made her happier and
more content, but enabled her to counteract the
restlessness of others that would inevitably have
brought misery upon themselves and all around
them.

One day, towards the close of the summer,
when the court had left Winchester, and Hilda
was at home once more, Gurth went into her
bower where she sat with her embroidery, and
after relating all the news, stood watching his
sister's patient efforts to disentangle some silks
and worsteds.

"The world is somewhat like thy silk, Hilda,"
he said, after a pause.

"What, so tangled and tumbled that none
can straighten it? Nay, nay, God will make it
straight, I doubt not. Look at this," she said,
holding up the reverse side of the tapestry she
was working. "What dost thou see?"

"A worse tangle, and many loose threads that
would puzzle me sorely to understand," said
Gurth with a smile.

"Well, I have been thinking much of this

WORSTEDS: *strands of woolen yarn*

needlework of late—thinking that it may be somewhat like God's work in the world. We can only see the back of it now, and it is all tangled and confused and without seeming order, but He who bids us put in our little stitches one at a time hath clear in His mind what the pattern shall be even from the beginning; and seeing the end from the beginning, there can be no mistake in God's work."

"Little sister, I wish I could believe as thou dost," said Sir Gurth.

"Believe Gytha's message that 'God is love'? nay, but thou dost believe it, Gurth," said Hilda eagerly.

"Not as thou dost, Hilda. I can believe He is loving and good to thee; but for England, for the world—" and the young man shook his head sadly.

A few weeks later and the brother and sister were at Winchester again, and, marvel of marvels, went to church, or rather to the cathedral, together, to hear good Bishop Aldred preach—Aldred their own Saxon prelate, who had urged Earl Harold to accept the crown of England, and afterwards placed it on his brow in the new Westminster. Preaching was not an everyday occurrence then. People went to mass, and there the matter ended, so that the news of this sermon brought many together, and Gurth declared afterwards he would not have missed hearing it for anything, though it was strangely like what Hilda had learned from her embroidery.

"We in the dust and din of the battle cannot hope to see or understand much beyond the groanings and wailings that fill our ears, but He who is King of all the earth and all the ages can see through the dimness and darkness of this time; and though He bids His servants dry the falling tears, and soothe the pain of all the sufferers now, it is 'the beyond' He looks at. He who gave His Son to redeem the world, will not let it be lost now, for He is still love—yes, 'God is love,'" concluded the venerable bishop, quoting Gytha's message; and Hilda, to whom it had brought such joy and blessing, whispered to her brother as they left the cathedral, "Yes, 'God is love,' and we are to show it to each other."

"Thou hast done it, and thou art doing it still, for what is our home—'our refuge and house of peace,' as my mother calls it—but the memorial of Gytha's message?" said her brother.

"And such it shall ever be," said Hilda.

And such it ever was. One of the few holdings given to a Saxon, Sir Gurth held it as a house of peace, a refuge for the desolate and oppressed, where his sister and her faithful bower-maiden tried to teach each newcomer the lesson we in these later times are still learning amid doubts and difficulties—to trust in God, and believe that He doeth all things well for the world, and for each soul that seeks to know Him.

The End

ABOUT THE AUTHOR

Emma Leslie (1837-1909), whose actual name was Emma Dixon, lived in Lewisham, Kent, in the south of England. She was a prolific Victorian children's author who wrote over 100 books. Emma Leslie's first book, *The Two Orphans*, was published in 1863 and her books remained in print for years after her death. She is buried at the St. Mary's Parish Church, in Pwllcrochan, Pembroke, South Wales.

Emma Leslie brought a strong Christian emphasis into her writing and many of her books were published by the Religious Tract Society. Her extensive historical fiction works covered many important periods in church history. Her writing also included a short booklet on the life of Queen Victoria published in the 50th year of the Queen's reign.

Emma Leslie Church History Series

GLAUCIA THE GREEK SLAVE
A Tale of Athens in the First Century
After the death of her father, Glaucia is sold to a wealthy Roman family to pay his debts. She tries hard to adjust to her new life but longs to find a God who can love even a slave. Meanwhile, her brother, Laon, struggles to find her and to earn enough money to buy her freedom. But what is the mystery that surrounds their mother's disappearance years earlier and will they ever be able to read the message in the parchments she left for them?

THE CAPTIVES
Or, Escape from the Druid Council
The Druid priests are as cold and cruel as the forest spirits they claim to represent, and Guntra, the chief of her tribe of Britons, must make a desperate deal with them to protect those she loves. Unaware of Guntra's struggles, Jugurtha, her son, longs to drive the hated Roman conquerors from the land. When he encounters the Christian centurion, Marcinius, Jugurtha mocks the idea of a God of love and kindness, but there comes a day when he is in need of love and kindness for himself and his beloved little sister. Will he allow Marcinius to help him? And will the gospel of Jesus Christ ever penetrate the brutal religion of the proud Britons?

OUT OF THE MOUTH OF THE LION
Or, The Church in the Catacombs
When Flaminius, a high Roman official, takes his wife, Flavia, to the Colosseum to see Christians thrown to the lions, he has no idea the effect it will have. Flavia cannot forget the faith of the martyrs, and finally, to protect her from complete disgrace or even danger, Flaminius requests a transfer to a more remote government post. As he and his family travel to the seven cities of Asia Minor mentioned in Revelation, he sees the various responses of the churches to persecution. His attitude toward the despised Christians begins to change, but does he dare forsake the gods of Rome and embrace the Lord Jesus Christ?

www.SalemRidgePress.com

EMMA LESLIE CHURCH HISTORY SERIES

SOWING BESIDE ALL WATERS
A Tale of the World in the Church
There is newfound freedom from persecution for Christians under the emperor, Constantine, but newfound troubles as well. Errors and pagan ways are creeping into the Church, while many of the most devoted Christians are withdrawing from the world into the desert as hermits and nuns. Quadratus, one of the emperor's special guards, is concerned over these developments, even in his own family. Then a riot sweeps through the city and Quadratus' home is ransacked. When he regains consciousness, he finds that his sister, Placidia, is gone. Where is she? And can the Church handle the new freedom, and remain faithful?

FROM BONDAGE TO FREEDOM
A Tale of the Times of Mohammed
At a Syrian market two Christian women are sold as slaves. One of the slaves ends up in Rome where Bishop Gregory is teaching his new doctrine of "purgatory" and the need for Christians to finish paying for their own sins. The other slave travels with her new master, Mohammed, back to Arabia, where Mohammed eventually declares himself to be the prophet of God. In Rome and Arabia, the two women and countless others fall into the bondage of man-made religions—will they learn at last to find true freedom in the Lord Jesus Christ alone?

THE MARTYR'S VICTORY
A Story of Danish England
Knowing full well they may die in the attempt, a small band of monks sets out to convert the savage Danes who have laid waste to the surrounding countryside year after year. The monks' faith is sorely tested as they face opposition from the angry Priest of Odin as well as doubts, sickness and starvation, but their leader, Osric, is unwavering in his attempts to share the "White Christ" with those who reject Him. Then the monks discover a young Christian woman who has escaped being sacrificed to the Danish gods—can she help reach those who had enslaved her and tried to kill her?

www.SalemRidgePress.com

Additional Titles Available From

Salem Ridge Press

YUSSUF THE GUIDE
*Being the Strange Story of the Travels in Asia Minor of
Burne the Lawyer, Preston the Professor, and
Lawrence the Sick*
by George Manville Fenn
Illustrated by John Schönberg

Young Lawrence, an invalid, convinces his guardians, Preston the Professor and Burne the Lawyer, to take him along on an archaeological expedition to Turkey. Before they set out, they engage Yussuf as their guide. Through the months that follow, the friends travel deeper and deeper into the remote regions of central Turkey on their trusty horses in search of ancient ruins. Yussuf proves his worth time and time again as they face dangers from a murderous ship captain, poisonous snakes, sheer precipices, bands of robbers and more. Memorable characters, humor and adventure abound in this exciting story!

MARIE'S HOME
Or, A Glimpse of the Past
by Caroline Austin
Illustrated by Gordon Browne R. I.

Eleven-year-old Marie Hamilton and her family travel to France at the invitation of Louis XVI, just before the start of the French Revolution. There they encounter the tremendous disparity between the proud French Nobility and the oppressed and starving French people. When an enraged mob storms the palace of Versailles, Marie and her family are rescued from grave danger by a strange twist of events, but Marie's story of courage, self-sacrifice and true nobility is not yet over! Honor, duty, compassion and forgiveness are all portrayed in this uplifting story.

www.SalemRidgePress.com

For Younger Readers

DOWN THE SNOW STAIRS
Or, From Goodnight to Goodmorning
by Alice Corkran
Illustrated by Gordon Browne R. I.
On Christmas Eve, eight-year-old Kitty cannot sleep, knowing that her beloved little brother is critically ill due to her own disobedience. Traveling in a dream to Naughty Children Land, she meets many strange people, including Daddy Coax and Lady Love. Kitty longs to return to the Path of Obedience but can she resist the many temptations she faces? Will she find her way home in time for Christmas? An imaginative and delightful read-aloud for the whole family!

SOLDIER FRITZ
A Story of the Reformation
by Emma Leslie
Illustrated by C. A. Ferrier
Young Fritz wants to follow in the footsteps of Martin Luther and be a soldier for the Lord, so he chooses a Bible from the peddler's pack as his birthday gift. When his father, the Count, goes off to war, however, Fritz and his mother and little sister are forced to flee into the forest to escape being thrown in prison for their new faith. Disguising themselves as commoners, they must trust the Lord as they wait and hope for the Count to rescue them. But how will he ever be able to find them?

AMERICAN TWINS OF THE REVOLUTION
Written and illustrated by Lucy Fitch Perkins
General Washington has no money to pay his discouraged troops and twins Sally and Roger are asked by their father, General Priestly, to help hide a shipment of gold which will be used to pay the American soldiers. Unfortunately, British spies have also learned about the gold and will stop at nothing to prevent it from reaching General Washington. Based on a true story, this is a thrilling episode from our nation's history!

www.SalemRidgePress.com

Historical Fiction by William W. Canfield

THE WHITE SENECA
Illustrated by G. A. Harker

Captured by the Senecas, fifteen-year-old Henry Cochrane grows to love the Indian ways and becomes Dundiswa—the White Seneca. When Henry is captured by an enemy tribe, however, he must make a desperate attempt to escape from them and rescue fellow captive, Constance Leonard. He will need all the skills he has learned from the Indians, as well as great courage and determination, if he is to succeed. But what will happen to the young woman if they do reach safety? And will he ever be able to return to his own people?

AT SENECA CASTLE
Illustrated by G. A. Harker

In this sequel to *The White Seneca*, Henry Cochrane, now eighteen, faces many perils as he serves as a scout for the Continental Army. General Washington is determined to do whatever it takes to stop the constant Indian attacks on the settlers and yet Henry is torn between his love for the Senecas and his loyalty to his own people. As the Army advances across New York State, Henry receives permission to travel ahead and warn his Indian friends of the coming destruction. But will he reach them in time? And what has happened to the beautiful Constance Leonard whom he had been forced to leave in captivity a year earlier?

THE SIGN ABOVE THE DOOR

Young Prince Martiesen is ruler of the land of Goshen in Egypt, where the Hebrews live. Eight plagues have already come upon Egypt and now Martiesen has been forced by Pharaoh to further increase the burden of the Hebrews. Martiesen, however, is in love with the beautiful Hebrew maiden, Elisheba, whom he is forbidden by Egyptian law to marry. As the nation despairs, the other nobles turn to Martiesen for leadership, but before he can decide what to do, Elisheba is kidnapped by the evil Peshala and terrifying darkness falls over the land. An exciting tale woven around the events of the Exodus from the Egyptian perspective!

www.SalemRidgePress.com